# LIBERTY AND DESTINTY

## A NOVEL OF THE AMERICAN REVOLUTION

JESSICA JAMES

**Liberty and Destiny**

**Liberty and Destiny was a 2014 Valley Forge Romance Writers Sheila Award Finalist.**

Printed in the USA

🌸 Created with Vellum

# CHAPTER 1

*The cunning of the fox is as murderous as the violence of the wolf; and we ought to guard equally against both.*
- Thomas Paine, The Crises

Colonel Grant Morgan continued writing even as the sound of muffled voices and footsteps advanced in the hallway. His gaze shifted and fell upon the crumpled message lying on the desk before him, causing his jaw to tighten and his brow to crease with agitation. Returning to his work, he casually pulled a nearby book onto the paper, hiding the communication from view.

When the door opened, he barely glanced at the woman standing between the two guards—but it was long enough for his heart to sink with disappointment and resentment. The young lady was the same one he had often seen talking to British officers. He'd only noticed her because of her beauty. But no amount of loveliness or grace could make up for the fact that she was apparently a Loyalist—or worse yet, a traitor.

"It was necessary to bind her hands?" He addressed the question to the guards, but had already turned his attention back to his paperwork.

"She warned us she'd fight like the devil," one of the men answered. "We thought it best."

Morgan lifted his eyes, but this time, not his head. "Is this true?"

The woman, though obviously weary from her journey, stood with a straight back and an unwavering glare. Her expression was one of angry defiance, and her dark eyes flashed with sparks of outrage. "I gave fair warning that I will fight against this vile intrusion. By whose authority do I suffer this indignity?"

Colonel Morgan stopped her with an impatient wave of his hand, but did not bother to answer. Nodding toward the door, he dismissed the two guards before going back to his paperwork. Though acutely aware of the woman standing before him, he pretended to be preoccupied while waiting for the men to depart. After the latch clicked shut behind the last soldier, he began to question her, but did not cease his writing. "Do you understand why you have been brought here?"

He heard the woman take a step closer to his desk. "I assume you received a communication about me."

Morgan stopped writing in mid-sentence and raised his eyes with a questioning look. "What do you know of the communication I received and how do you know it?"

"I wrote it," she replied matter-of-factly, her tone no longer hostile.

Colonel Morgan put down the quill and leaned forward, making no attempt to disguise his surprise. "You wrote a communication implicating yourself as a spy?"

"Yes, sir." She took another step forward so she now

stood right in front of his desk. Her voice was soft, little more than a whisper. "I needed to speak to you, and I could devise no other way to come here without raising suspicion."

"Raising suspicion? Miss, you are speaking in riddles. Why would you need to speak to *me* and in such a manner?"

"Sir, I reside at the Spangler house, near Smithtown."

"I see." The words were said with a mixture of disdain and discontent. It was just as he thought. The residents of the house were well known for their loyalty to the Crown—so much so that British officers often used the home as their headquarters when they occupied the region.

"I am in a position to—" She paused and swallowed hard as if she'd lost her nerve, but then hastily recovered. "To overhear certain things… and I have reason to believe you have a spy within your ranks. Close to you."

Morgan stood and leaned across his desk in one movement. "How dare you make such an accusation. What would possess you to say such a thing?"

"I cannot divulge how I know." She stood before him with lowered head, her hands still bound behind her back. "Yet I can tell you they are aware of your movements, your troop numbers, and your plans." Her tone was even and quiet with just a hint of desperation in it.

Morgan strode to the fireplace and poked a moment at the smoky logs as he thought about her accusation. Despite his best attempts at secrecy, many of his efforts at reconnaissance had ended in a skirmish rather than intelligence gained. It did indeed seem as if the British sensed where he was going to be and when.

He glanced back at the disheveled woman standing by his desk and scrutinized her more closely. Her hair appeared unruly as if it had been combed by the wind. Her eyes showed immense fatigue. Why would she go to such extremes to seek him if she wasn't telling the truth?

"I have no reason to distrust or suspect anyone close to me." Morgan turned to face her. "It would be foolish of me, don't you think, to take the word of a perfect stranger? A Loyalist, no less?"

He watched her eyes fill with tears before she turned her head to keep him from seeing them.

"Why are you crying?" he asked with a severe tone, although his heart melted at the sight.

"I knew there was little chance you would believe me."

"Yet still you came?"

She inhaled a ragged breath. "The lives at stake… the treachery. I had to come." She lowered her head and murmured. "I could think of no other way."

Morgan walked to her, and put a finger upon her cheek, stopping a tear before it slid down her face. "The moisture is real enough," he said under his breath. "I wonder about the claim."

She did not respond other than to gaze up at him with large, fawn-like eyes that glistened unnaturally with deep pools of liquid not yet spilled. Long, dark lashes blinked them back from behind wisps of hair straying wildly from an upswept coiffure. Her appearance seemed to confirm that his men had followed his order to make haste during the ride.

Morgan turned away, unable to face the innocent countenance peering up at him. She did not beg and bawl as most women in her situation would have, yet he still could not bring himself to believe her. These days it was impossible to decipher friend from foe. You just couldn't tell about people these days. Not even women.

Least of all, beautiful ones.

"You have placed me in an awkward position, Miss…" He glanced back to his desk for the note she had written.

"Adair."

"Yes, Miss Adair. Just how is it that you came to reside at the Spangler house? The proprietor there is—"

"Charles Spangler." She looked down at her feet. "My uncle."

"I see," Morgan said, rubbing his chin.

The young lady swallowed hard and her lips trembled as she talked. "My parents died when I was five. I have resided there most of my life." She shifted her weight as if uncomfortable. "Not of my wanting, I assure you."

"They are Loyalists?"

Her eyes remained cast on the floor, quiet and calm. "My uncle is a merchant. Trading with the British is his livelihood."

"And yet you oppose the occupation?" He took a step closer.

When she looked up her eyes were steady in their gaze of him. "I believe my country is more important than individual wealth or power, that men should fight for principle not gain." She shrugged, but he detected something brave in her spirit, something penetrating in her eye, before her focus returned to the floor. "That is all."

Morgan sat on the edge of his desk and crossed his arms. "Miss Adair, your story is intriguing, yet, you must admit, a bit incredible."

"The risk is real, Colonel Morgan," she replied defiantly. "The time to act is now."

"And yet I see neither the expediency nor the necessity, quite frankly," he said. "Unless, of course, you can show me something that would prove I should believe you."

The young woman swallowed hard and stared for a moment at the fire, giving him time to study her face. Her countenance appeared youthful and alive, yet weary and drawn as she paused to ponder his question. It was an innocent-looking, fresh face, yet somehow it spoke of wisdom and reason.

After a few long moments, she tilted her head back, exposing white flesh above her collar. She looked at him with serious intent. "I have nothing but this."

Morgan took a step closer. "And just what is that?" He stared at her in confusion.

"It is my neck, of course," she said in a quiet voice. "The only one in my possession. And I have placed it in great danger by coming here."

Morgan threw up his hands as he walked back to the fire and began to pace. If the girl's accusations were true, he had to begin this instant to find the informant. If he discovered she was lying, he still had her in his possession to punish as necessary. It appeared he held all the cards.

He turned back to her. "Why do you think this spy, this informant, is close to me?" He walked to his desk, sat upon it with his arms crossed, and examined her as she spoke, watching closely for any evidence of hesitation or doubt.

"As I said, he has been reporting your numbers, your movements and your plans."

"Such as?"

"You have boasted of three companies, but your numbers reveal less than two." She paused as if unsure she should continue. "You have recently been supplied with a cannon, along with two dozen—"

In one movement, Morgan banged his fist on the desk and stood. "How do you know this?"

"It is not me you should be worried about," she said determinedly. "It is the British."

Morgan started pacing again, ignoring the girl as he angrily pondered who could have betrayed him. He came to an abrupt stop in front of her, deciding he had other things to take care of first. "But why are you *here*? What possessed you to come to *me*?"

She had been staring out the window, but his voice commanded her to look at him. Her eyes began to glisten as she gazed up at him. "You are foremost in resisting royal authority in the south. That is why the British wish to stop you."

"Go on," he said when she paused.

"I came because it is my duty to throw the weight of my arm—however feeble—onto the scale for the cause of liberty." Her chin trembled and she appeared about to cry again before she turned away. "It is that simple."

"War is never simple," Morgan grumbled, staring at her back. He raked a hand through his hair in irritation. He had a campaign to plan. Yet now he was faced with a dilemma that could well doom that campaign to failure if he did not act. If she was lying, he would be wasting precious time. But if she were not…

"Tell me, Miss Adair, what do you suggest I do with you?"

She shrugged, making it clear she had not made plans for anything past this moment. "That is no business of mine to solve." She turned around to face him. "What would you do with any prisoner with whom you had suspicion?"

He laughed and then gazed at her with a skeptical look. "I would imprison such a person, and question them at length over a duration of days."

"Then you have your answer," she said. "The British—and the man within your ranks who is working with them—must believe I am being held here against my will."

Colonel Morgan stood in front of her and bent down so his eyes were even with hers. "You believe that we Patriots are so uncivilized we would imprison a *woman*?"

She remained calm but defiant. "Woman or not, the

harm I could inflict as a spy would be no less than that of a man. True?"

Morgan sighed heavily, walked away, and leaned his hands for a moment on the mantle over the fireplace as he considered his next move. At the age of twenty-five, he had been leading the life of a gentleman with easy deeds and no great responsibility. And now, at twenty-eight, he was in command of a large band of men, enduring daily discomfort, and having to make life and death decisions on behalf of his country. His keen sense of duty compelled him to do so willingly—but having to deal with a woman was another matter entirely.

"You have all the right answers," he finally said, looking back over his shoulder. "But can I believe you?"

Her eyes flicked over to his, yet she made no comment other than what he read plainly in her expression. For the first time, she appeared dejected and broken as if she had reached the end of her endurance. She had borne the journey with commendable fortitude, but now a dark weariness settled over her, stealing the color from her face and the life from her eyes.

"Believe what you will," she said at last, shrugging and looking down, her hair falling across her face. "I have said what I came to say. I can do no more."

Morgan cocked his head and stared at her. She was young, not yet twenty and one he guessed. Yet she had a wisdom and wit resembling one thrice her years. How remarkable that she would renounce extravagance and comfort for the sake of patriotic duty—if she were indeed telling the truth. He had to be careful though.

"Now that you have started this charade, I fear it must continue until the culprit is found." He walked toward her as he deliberated upon his options. "And I'm afraid you will find our camp hospitality somewhat wanting in comfort. It will not be pleasant."

"I knew that coming here would mean hardship and adversity," came the solemn response. She did not bother to raise her eyes, and spoke as if forming words required much effort. "But not coming could mean something much worse for my country."

Morgan cocked his head again, trying to detect any sign of treachery or deceit. He saw only sincerity, with no hint of fright or uncertainty. She appeared somewhat childlike and feminine, yet had a solid aspect of hardened steel about her. Even when staring straight ahead, which was most of the time, he could tell her mind was not idle—nor was it fretful.

"Still, I am reluctant to put you through it."

The tone of his voice perhaps, more so than the words, made her meet his gaze squarely. "No trials could be more difficult than those through which I have already passed." She removed her attention from him and stared out the window again as if that was all she was going to say on the subject.

The expression of calm courage made his pulse quicken. "You appear to possess a patriot's heart, Miss Adair, yet I can't help but wonder if it will be worth the cost."

"If you find the traitor, it will be worth the cost." She spoke with calm assurance, but did not bother to remove her distant gaze from the window.

Morgan recognized a conviction and sincerity in her manner that somewhat silenced his reservations and mistrust, but still he worried about her ability to endure a night in captivity. He was soon relieved of that misgiving as well, for despite her obvious fatigue, her countenance reflected cool courage and commitment. Something in her deep brown eyes spoke of defiance, strong will, and strength.

He turned away, and cleared his throat. "To be clear, you expect no special consideration?"

"Treat me as if you believe I am a traitor," she replied steadily. "I understand the necessity of playing the game until the end."

"This is hardly a game," he said, turning back to her. "Do you expect payment for your services?"

He watched the color rise in her cheeks. "Liberty for my country is payment enough for me." She raised her head a notch higher as if insulted by the insinuation.

Morgan felt a vague sense of awe, and then one of painful apprehension, as he took in her motionless figure. The acceptance of her fate radiated in her eyes, but her face was destitute of all other expression. Never was anything so frail, and yet so very determined and resolute.

"You could not have found a person to whom your plan is more disagreeable," he said gravely under his breath. When she did not answer, nor change her vacant look, he strode toward the door, but turned back to her though before hailing the guards. "I apologize in advance for your treatment."

"She is a prisoner," he said to the men who entered. "You can unbind her hands. She has given her word." The soldiers nodded, but one paused and motioned to Morgan. "The holding cell, sir?"

"Yes, the holding cell."

Instead of watching her leave, Morgan turned back to his desk and listened to the door latch closed behind him.

# CHAPTER 2

*Those who expect to reap the blessings of freedom, must, like men,
undergo the fatigue of supporting it.*
- THOMAS PAINE

When a soldier came to take Sophia to Colonel Morgan the next day, she could not escape the chill coursing through her. The night had been a long one, spent in a cold, damp cellar so devoid of light, it had been impossible to tell if her eyes were open or closed. The guards had done nothing to improve her miserable conditions other than toss her an extra blanket. The thin, threadbare cloth had offered little comfort and done nothing to keep out the cold.

Upon entering the same room where she'd met Colonel Morgan the day before, Sophia pulled back the hood of her cloak. The illumination of the sun coming through the window on one side, and the blazing fire on the other made her blink repeatedly, contrasting as it did with the darkness to which her eyes were accustomed.

When things came into focus, she saw Colonel Morgan at his desk again, his quill pen scratching noisily across a piece of paper. He shot her a cursory glance from behind his desk before dismissing the guard with a wave of his hand. Sophia heard the door close behind her and waited for the colonel's attention, but he had already returned to his work.

Shivering and miserable, she edged her way over to the fireplace, and allowed the heat to sink into her aching bones. Since the colonel seemed unaware of her presence, she studied him as he turned to another stack of papers. He looked out of place in the neat, orderly room. His shirt was tucked negligently into the waistband of a pair of buckskin riding breeches, and his breeches were tucked into a pair of mud-splattered boots. Sophia's gaze flitted from his massive form to his coat lying haphazardly on a chair beside him, appearing to have been flung there in a moment of great impatience and hurry.

He sat in a relaxed manner, with the sleeves of his linen shirt rolled up to his elbows. But even with his informal appearance, he gave the impression of authoritative command, possessing a certain dignity that reflected both power and strength. It had taken only one meeting for her to conclude that he was a man whose merit equaled his reputation.

Sophia felt like she almost knew him, so often had she heard the British soldiers mention his name. His zeal for the cause, and his complete disregard of personal danger had procured him a reputation distinct from all others. By his bold offensive decisions, he had succeeded in arresting the British movements, making his name synonymous with victory.

Yet, from what she'd heard, this was a position thrust

upon him, not *sought* by him. Raised on a thriving plantation, he was a gentleman by birth, and became a soldier out of necessity and patriotism.

Sophia studied him closer as the fire spit and crackled behind her, slowly eliminating the chill from her bones. He was, as she had pictured, a formidable and intimidating-looking man, someone you knew at once had to be taken seriously.

His eyes struck her as the most noticeable feature of all. Although not of a stunning hue, they were mysterious, dark orbs whose color was hard to describe. Not quite blue, nor yet gray—they instead reflected a deep blending of the two. Intense and overpowering, they revealed nothing as far as emotion—and everything as far as a restless sense of duty.

Sophia tilted her head and squinted as if that would help her scrutiny of him. In all of the stories she had heard of his military prowess, never had anyone mentioned how conspic-uously striking he appeared. His natural dark complexion, deepened by exposure to sun and wind, made him appear quite handsome—if one were to notice such things…

Sophia tore her eyes away and focused them instead out the window. No doubt, any number of women had.

A loud *tap, tap, tap* of approaching footsteps from the hallway diverted Sophia's attention. Within moments, the latch clicked open, and a neatly-dressed officer stood breathing heavily on the threshold. He looked at Colonel Morgan, who raised his eyes from the work, and then to Sophia, with a perusal so thorough it made her blush. When no one said anything, he asked brusquely, "For what was the lady brought?"

Colonel Morgan's gaze traveled over to Sophia as if just realizing she was there. Then he leaned back in his chair while tapping a quill pen on the desk. "You will kindly close the door, Captain Tate?"

The officer stepped in and pushed the door closed behind him.

"I intended to wait for the others to arrive, but since you have asked, she's a Tory." Morgan's tone was low and grave. "Brought here on suspicion of providing information to the British."

"By whose authority?" the man asked.

Morgan cocked his head to one side and gazed at the captain curiously. "On *my* authority, of course."

The man threw his hat carelessly onto the desk and smiled. "That is obvious, Grant. I meant to say, what is the evidence against her?"

Sophia blinked at the lack of formality on the part of the newly arrived officer. He and Colonel Morgan appeared to be good friends, yet the difference in them was quite remarkable. Captain Tate was handsome enough, with an aristocratic and well-bred deportment, but he dressed frivolously and with obvious care—making him appear a bit foppish.

Colonel Morgan on the other hand wore a uniform destitute of strap or chevron to indicate even the humblest rank. The coat, which he had finally donned from the chair and was buttoning with great impatience, appeared threadbare and mottled from heavy use.

"I'll present the details when the other officers arrive," Morgan responded. "Tea while we wait?"

Sophia stepped aside as he pulled the arm of the kettle away from the fire.

"Would you like some hot tea, Miss Adair?"

Colonel Morgan spoke with effortless good manners, but Sophia assumed his formality indicated mistrust, rather than respect. She nodded, and then tried to make a reasonable response. "Just a l-little," she said at last, trying without success to keep her teeth from chattering.

"You look half-frozen." Captain Tate stepped forward

and, after preparing a saucer, handed it to Sophia while bowing low. "I hope Colonel Morgan has not been overly unkind to you, Miss Adair. You must not judge us on his actions alone."

Sophia accepted his offering with a nod, but did not trust herself to speak. The man appeared self-confident and relaxed, yet something about him made her keep up her guard.

A quick knock was followed by the entrance of five more men, all of whom loudly clanked their muddy boots at the door. When they looked up and noticed Sophia, they removed their hats in unison, but the action seemed more of a force of habit from gentlemen than one of respect for her in particular.

"Come in, men." Colonel Morgan talked while clasping his last coat button. "I see you received my message."

Judging from their silent and hasty entrance, punctuality was rigidly enforced in Morgan's command. As they filed in, two of them took chairs while the others crossed their arms and leaned against the wide windowsills. Sophia could see these were men of good blood—not aristocrats—but farmers and businessmen. These were men who didn't seek trouble, yet they possessed a demeanor that told her they would know what to do if they found it.

Although a few of them looked very young, all appeared to be hardened veterans of hazardous service. Their resolve was evident in the way they carried themselves, and the unflinching expression of intrepidity upon their faces made it obvious they would not balk from performing the service asked of them.

She shifted her gaze to study each man in the ragged group and noted the desperate state of their attire. They appeared sorely in need of everything—warm coats, leggings, and shoes. But the determination stamped on their faces showed Sophia that patriotism and purpose would keep them in camp no matter the privations they were forced to endure.

After they had settled, all of their gazes rested upon Sophia—with noticeable disfavor. The contempt in which they beheld her was palpable, making it hard not to weaken beneath their withering glares. Captain Tate alone seemed to harbor no resentment, his expression appearing somewhat sympathetic to her plight.

"Gentlemen, as I said in my message to you, Miss Adair was brought in on suspicion of passing information to the British." Morgan stood in front of his men, holding the correspondence in his hand. "As I have no real evidence against her, I wished to seek your opinion on what should be done."

Sophia's gaze flitted back to Colonel Morgan, and she couldn't help but notice that even among men of equal daring, he appeared a man apart. Armed with little more than honor and courage, he had assembled this group of countrymen, formed them into a militia, and led them against a vastly superior force with notable and distinguished success. It was apparent from the way they regarded him that the gallant young officer had won their unbounded admiration.

"You said you received a communication about her," one of the men said. "That's evidence, isn't it?"

"It was not signed," Morgan said as he lowered himself onto the edge of his desk. "I cannot consider that as evidence, surely."

"And what does the lady say?" another asked.

Colonel Morgan glanced at Sophia, but continued the conversation as if she were not present. "She denies all charges, of course."

"But she lives at the Spangler house, doesn't she?" A man

with tattered-looking pants and noticeable holes in his shoes glared at her. "That is reason enough to assume she is a Tory!"

Another officer, a heavy man with a grizzly beard, stood and waved his hand in the air. "A line of distinction must be drawn between soldiers taken in battle and spies taken in action. The first are prisoners, but the latter, traitors. The one forfeits liberty, the other, his—or her—head."

"Hold your tongue, Beck." A man, somewhat older than the others, began pacing in an irritated manner. He possessed a weatherworn face, deeply lined, but his eyes showed a father's patience. He appeared to be the type of man who spoke little, but who was listened to when he did.

"We cannot hold her just because she resides in a Tory house. We cannot sink to the level of our enemy, whose tactics we abhor."

"I concur," another said with a thoughtful expression. "Yet what if she is a spy? A traitor? Woman or not, she should be punished."

"I move that we send her back across the lines at the first opportunity."

All eyes turned to Captain Tate, who had spoken the words. "We have no means of holding a woman," he said in a self-confident voice. "Look at her. She spent a single night in our unhealthy accommodations. How many more could she even endure?"

Though she knew she was the center of attention, Sophia tried to appear indifferent and unaffected, by staring straight ahead.

The man named Beck responded with an angry wave of his hand. "I've no doubt she wouldn't last long, her life being softened by the comfort provided by the enemy during a time of war—at the cost of *our* liberty!"

"Are we to live with the blood of an innocent on our hands?" Tate shot back. "I do not believe she is a spy."

Sophia felt her cheeks grow warm as all of the men studied her. Lowering her gaze, she noticed that her cloak was streaked with dirt, probably her face as well. Her hair, which had been neatly styled before her journey, was now hanging in clumps upon her shoulders. She cast her eyes toward the window across the room and sighed deeply, wishing herself away from this place.

"And just how did you draw such a conclusion?" the man named Beck growled.

"I draw no conclusions, sir," Tate answered lazily, "but rely on known and visible facts. Look at her, and tell me I am in error."

Sophia continued listening to the men while trying to appear uninterested. It was difficult considering she was the sole topic of the conversation and the object of so much scrutiny.

"Can the lady speak?"

Startled, Sophia turned to the man who addressed her. "Of course I can speak, and thank you for the kindness of acknowledging my presence."

"No need to get your hackles up, Miss Adair. This is serious business, and needs to be—"

"Serious business indeed when a woman is kidnapped in broad daylight," she replied with a tilt of her head, playing her part by radiating angry defiance.

"Not kidnapped," Colonel Morgan said. "Brought in for questioning. And you *were* riding near our outpost."

Sophia put her face in her hands and began to sob. "But I've done nothing wrong, save live among English gentle-men." She raised her head and pretended to blink back tears. "And *they* do not make war on gentlewomen."

"Now, now Miss Adair." Captain Tate stepped forward.

"Colonel Morgan had to bring you in. I'm sure you understand."

"But he has no evidence," Sophia cried. "Ask him if it is so."

The room fell quiet for a moment. "It is so," he finally said without being asked.

"Please, you can't allow them to put me back in that dreadful cell." She took a step toward Captain Tate, as he seemed to be the most lenient, and appeared to possess some authority over the other men. "Have mercy on me."

Tate turned to the others. "What say you, men? Are your hearts so cold that you will allow an innocent woman to suffer?"

Sophia's eyes, seemingly of their own accord, fell upon Colonel Morgan, who stood contemplating her with an expression of empathy mixed with suspicion. She hadn't not anticipated that he would rely on the will of his men to decide her fate.

"No one said she is *innocent*," he said at last in a grave tone. "We possess no evidence one way or the other."

"I say we send her back and good riddance," the heavy-set man said. "We got no place to hold her except for that old root cellar, and she'd be nothin' but trouble if we kept her."

"Agreed," another mumbled, as others nodded their assent. "Though there is plenty of room for doubt."

"Yes." Morgan studied her intently. "And I am full of it."

"If you let her go, you're going to regret it," the man with the holes in his shoes said. "Mark my words."

Morgan sat and tapped his fingers on the desk, while studying Sophia with impassive eyes. "Consider them marked."

Sophia tried to determine whether he was acting the part or truly still had doubts about her sincerity. Reading nothing from his inscrutable expression, she turned her attention back to the view out the window and waited for his next move.

"Very well," Morgan said at last. "There are a few more questions I'd like to ask Miss Adair, but I'll allow you gentlemen to get back to your duties."

"I'd be glad to stay," Captain Tate offered, looking up at Colonel Morgan and smiling.

"That won't be necessary," Morgan said tersely. "You are dismissed."

Seeming to ignore the order, Captain Tate walked over to Sophia and bowed. "Allow me to express my regrets that mere suspicions have put you in such material discomfort."

When Sophia started to speak he silenced her with his hand. "But however greatly I mourn the error for your sake, it is somewhat balanced by the pleasure you have afforded us by your presence." He took her hand and brought it to his lips. "I pray you will not judge all patriots by the actions of a few." He paused and gave a scornful glance toward Colonel Morgan.

Sophia batted her eyelashes as she had seen her cousin do in front of the British soldiers. "The captain is over-kind. I'm sure the memory of my imprisonment will be greatly improved by your kind and gracious words."

Sophia could feel Colonel Morgan's eyes burning into her with an intensity that was palpable. When Captain Tate finally disappeared out the door, she turned her back on Morgan, and warmed her hands by the fire in an effort to escape his withering gaze.

# CHAPTER 3

*The battle, sir, is not to the strong alone; it is to the vigilant, the active, the brave.*
- Patrick Henry, speech at the Virginia Convention, 1775

*A*fter Captain Tate had disappeared through the door, Colonel Morgan took Sophia's saucer of tea and refilled it with sophisticated grace.

"I trust the night passed not too disagreeably," he said handing it back to her. "I apologize for the accommodations."

Startled, Sophia lifted her head at the gentleness of his voice, trying to decide if he were being sincere or merely pretending to be concerned. As usual, his bronze face appeared indifferent and his eyes showed no hint of emotion. Although it had been the longest and most unpleasant night of her life, she simply shrugged and mumbled, "It was of my own accord. I have no cause to complain of any grievances here."

Morgan walked back to his desk and sipped at his tea while seeming to deliberate. "Well?" He turned at last and eyed her with a gaze that was as direct as it was intense.

Sophia stared at him confusedly, not sure of his meaning.

"Which one of these men do you believe is the culprit?"

Sophia took a deep breath as she pondered his question, realizing for the first time he had called his men in so *she* could scrutinize *them*—not the other way around as she had imagined.

"They treated me with obvious disdain—"

"I apologize," he said, coming to his feet. "You must understand, they—"

Sophia held up her hand. "As well they should, believing I am a spy."

The colonel sat down and remained silent, as if replaying the proceedings in his mind and assessing each man's behavior.

"There was but one who treated me with courtesy and seemed sympathetic to my plight."

Colonel Morgan burst out in laughter. "You cannot believe Captain Lawrence Tate is the traitor! A flirt perhaps —but a spy, never!"

Sophia shrugged. "I don't understand how you can be so sure."

"Because I *know* him—that is how." Morgan laughed again, and walked around to sit in his chair. "He is like a brother to me. Absolutely incapable of such treachery."

"But he is aware of your movements?"

He glanced up at her sharply. "Of course."

Sophia should have held her tongue rather than elaborate when she beheld the intensity of Morgan's gaze, but she did not. "You should not discard him so easily as the culprit," she said. "The informant must be very close to you."

Morgan stood and appeared to reach her in one stride, so quickly was he standing in front of her. "I would be more inclined to think *you* are a spy than Lawrence," he said pointing a finger in her face. "I value his friendship and beg you not to be the cause for forfeiting it."

Sophia took a step back at the sign of his hasty temper and the sheer physical force of the man. She stood perfectly still, afraid to move, afraid to look away, and almost afraid to breathe.

Morgan let his breath out slowly as if to regain his composure and returned to his desk. "Be that as it may," he said, staring at a pile of papers, "we now have the task of figuring out what to do with *you*. I've received no less than three communications from the British demanding your release." He turned to face her. "You seem to be held in quite high esteem by the Redcoats with whom you socialize."

Sophia felt the color rising in her cheeks, but said nothing, though she had to bite her tongue to accomplish it.

Morgan began flipping through some pages. "Yes, this one is especially interesting… from a Major Briggs." His flicked his gaze over the paper and then raised his eyes to meet hers. "Malcolm Briggs. A *special* acquaintance of yours?"

"I know him, yes." Sophia stared straight ahead, unable and unwilling to look into his searching eyes.

"I see," he said, expressively and with a hint of ridicule. "It says here he demands your release, or he will… let's see now, yes, here it is—wipe every last dirty ragtag Rebel off the face of the earth." He looked up with an inquisitive expression. "Quite elegant for an Englishman, don't you think?"

Sophia turned toward the fire and warmed her hands so he could not see her expression and try to read something from it. "I suppose he fancies me a damsel in distress. Englishmen are like that, you know."

When next Morgan spoke, he was standing directly behind her again, though she did not know how he accomplished it with such speed and stealth. "And what about Patriots?" His voice fell upon her ears soft and smooth. "Are we *incapable* of rescuing damsels in distress?"

Sophia turned around abruptly, and took a step back, even closer to the fire, due to his close proximity. "T-That's not what I meant," she stammered. When she looked up into his steady unnerving gaze, she could not conceive why this man had such an effect on her. Her presence seemed to be a matter of supreme indifference to him, yet here she was quaking beneath his scrutiny. "I meant that the British are adept at bluster—not necessarily action."

"Oh, I see." He smiled at her in a thoughtful, absorbed way—and she almost reached out for the back of a nearby chair to steady herself. The endearing smile made his face appear warm and comforting, no longer the restless warrior or intimidating officer he had resembled before.

But the smile did not last long. He took her arm and pulled her none too gently away from the fire. "You'll catch ablaze standing that close."

He walked back to his desk, sat, and became all business again. "I am sending you back through the lines under a flag of truce as requested by your...acquaintances." He paused and looked up as he said the last word as if for added effect, then returned to writing. "I am making it clear we do not hold prisoners based on hearsay, despite how our enemy treats such matters. It appears I have no other recourse since no evidence has been presented against you."

"Very well." Sophia turned to the fire once again to warm her hands.

"And there is one more thing."

Sophia glanced over her shoulder and waited for him to finish. He had stopped writing and sat staring at her as if once again trying to read her sincerity.

"The things you've seen here are not to be spoken of." He leaned forward to emphasize his point. "Do you honor me with that request?"

Somewhat confused, Sophia shrugged. "But what shall I tell them?"

The colonel cocked his head and looked at her sharply. "About what?"

Sophia walked over to his desk and sat down in the large chair in front of it. "About your numbers, weapons, and fortifications. They will ask me, of course."

Morgan's eyes turned a brilliant blue as he studied her with outraged scrutiny. "What are you suggesting? That I provide you with false intelligence?"

"It would seem strange if I returned having seen nothing, wouldn't it? Your men blindfolded me to bring me here through the swamp, but the walk to the cellar where I was held revealed—"

"Revealed what?" Morgan's voice rose with anger. "What is the game you are playing?"

Sophia sat before him calm and indifferent. "I couldn't help but notice the condition of the horses you possess and the fitness of your men for duty."

"And?" Morgan's dark eyes turned from blue to the color of a depthless stormy sea.

"Both appeared capable and battle ready." Sophia shrugged, though she was keenly aware of his intense appraisal. "So I would prefer that we decide what I should tell them."

Morgan put his palms on his desk and leaning forward as he did so. "What I've decided is that you've have gone too far." He straightened up and turned away. "Never would I agree to place such a burden on the shoulders of one so young and inexperienced."

He began to pace, his eyes on the floor as Sophia listened to the soft thud of his boots.

"I know these men. They will be eager to hear what I have to say, and take value in whatever I give them." She kept her voice calm as she tried to reason with him.

Morgan stopped and whirled around to face her. "I do not believe for an instant that you understand the danger of such an enterprise." He started pacing again as if not expecting a reply, but when she remained silent, he erupted. "Did you hear me?"

"Certainly I heard you. Your voice is sufficiently distinct." Sophia tried to meet his gaze, but could not stare long into his probing eyes. "To answer your question, I understand well the danger *and* the necessity."

"Well, tell me," he said, coming to a stop in front of her again and standing with his hands on his hips. "Just how much do you know about military affairs?"

This time she stood and did not turn away. "Not so much as you perhaps, but not so little as you think."

"What do you mean?"

"I have come a long way and at great peril to stand before you. Yet all I have done is nothing to the service I now have the power to render."

"You cannot be suggesting what I think you are suggesting!" Morgan turned and strode to the fireplace where he leaned his hands on the mantel. "This is not a game," he said, staring into the flames as he leaned forward. "These men are cunning."

"And you believe me incapable of such cunning?"

He sighed in exasperation, and looked over his shoulder at her. "That you are capable of cunning is becoming more apparent each minute, Miss Adair. It's your judgment I question."

Sophia shrugged and walked to the window. "I see no harm. The opportunity to mislead is evident. I think you are overly cautious."

Once again he turned his head to gaze at her, but this time he remained silent a moment. "If you think I am cautious, you little know me," he said at last.

The voice that fell upon Sophia's ears was solemn and serious. She watched a shadow cross his face before he turned back to the fireplace. Lifting his foot, he rolled one of the flaming logs which was tumbling forward back into the fire pit. His indifference to the danger was sufficiently surprising to her, but when the log broke under the weight of his boot still upon it, she took a startled step back.

Sophia knew she had misspoken about his prudence. She had often heard the British say that among the Patriots, there was not a single man of greater military grasp or one of more bold and audacious character. They talked of him as being a tireless, indomitable soldier, willing to take chances and always heedless of danger. His reputation for never backing down from a fight was amplified by the evidence that he often went out of his way to seek one.

Sophia had to admire him for the simple reason that the enemy, composed of trained and experienced soldiers, viewed him as a dangerous and talented rival, identifying his fearlessness as ferocity and his audacity as impudence.

"Just whom do you suppose they will blame when they discover your information is incorrect?" His voice sounded angry, yet was mixed with odd respect.

She scoffed at him. "Certainly they will think I was either naively mistaken or tricked by scheming Patriots."

Morgan sat and tapped his fingers on the desk violently as he studied her. Every glance from his inscrutable eyes now seemed driven forth as if on a special mission. "You seem to have this all worked out."

"I had a great deal of time to think about it last night," she responded curtly.

Sophia watched his eyes cloud over with skepticism and doubt, but could not determine if it was she he distrusted, or his own opinion. "I cannot ask you to do this," he finally said, shaking his head, leading her to believe it was the latter.

"You need not ask me," Sophia said firmly. "Just *let* me."

When he continued to stare at her with those deep, remorseless eyes, she began to expand on her plan. "What would the British do if I were to tell them it appeared you were preparing for a large move? And that I *overheard* someone mention an attack on the Tories at Woodsboro in a fortnight?"

He cocked his head as if analyzing her statement. "They would gather their forces and congregate at Woodsboro."

"Exactly." She nodded. "But they have no large force near to congregate there save those in Gladstone guarding the supply warehouses."

A slow smile began to spread across his face as he started to comprehend her strategy, but he quickly turned away. "So if I sent a small detachment to Woodsboro to lead them to believe your story was correct…"

"And the rest to Gladstone, you could overtake whatever small contingency they leave, and capture their stores and supplies." She said it matter-of-factly, as if the entire enterprise would be no more complicated than an afternoon picnic. "I believe it is a risk worth taking."

He looked at her, but no hint of a smile remained. "I am in the habit of making my own decisions," he said. "And forgive me for not being gullible, but it all seems a little too easy—like a British trap. How do I know Gladstone is not being reinforced as we speak?"

"I do not know, Colonel Morgan." Sophia threw her hands up in frustration. "You will just have to trust me."

"Ah, yes, just trust you." He studied her with a pensive stare, scrutinizing her so long she found it hard not to turn away.

But it was Colonel Morgan who finally lowered his searching gaze and turned his back. "I have a feeling I'm going to regret this."

Sophia tried not to let her breath escape with one long sigh of relief. "Why should you regret what you cannot control?"

He looked back over his shoulder briefly. "What I cannot control is exactly what I fear I will regret."

She scanned his face as he spoke, but before she had time to analyze his answer, he changed the subject. "It will delay your leaving, of course." His tone was a bit softer, though still formal, indicating he would brook no nonsense. "I need time to convey to my men that we will be making a demonstration on the Tories in Woodsboro. I'll split the force only after we are on our way so that no one will be tipped off ahead of time."

Sophia tried not to shiver at the thought of spending another night in the horrible cell.

Morgan continued talking as if he didn't notice. "Since we have been unable to prove that you've broken any laws, I will put you in a room at the Sully house." He looked at her gravely. "Under guard, of course."

Sophia nodded, grateful that he was gentleman enough not to make her endure another night in the cold cellar.

"Some of my men are quartered there," he continued, "so it's perfectly plausible you could overhear something."

She blinked in surprise, realizing it was not so much her comfort that prompted his actions, but rather that there be concrete evidence she could overhear a conversation about his plans.

"On what shall you blame the delay of my return?"

He looked over at her at the interruption, as he appeared to be still deep in thought. "We are preparing for a major move, Miss Adair. I don't have the time or the men to escort you back through the lines."

He said the words in a serious tone, but she thought she saw him wink before he returned to his desk, picked up a quill and began writing, never pausing or looking up until he was finished with his thought. Sophia was amazed at how calm and self-assured he appeared, as if it did not bother him in the least that the decisions he made today and the actions he would take tomorrow, could affect the nation for years, if not generations, to come.

When he had completed his task he looked up, and for a moment his gaze lingered in a stare so steadfast, so devouring that, try as she did not to look, her eyes were drawn to his. She could almost see him trying to read her soul, and at long last he seemed satisfied with what he saw and turned away.

"Now, if you'll excuse me, Miss Adair, I need to go find someone to escort you to the Sully house." He smiled, patting the paper on the desk twice with his hand before rising to leave.

By the time he got to the door, it seemed some doubts and trepidation had crept back into his mind. With his hand on the latch, he turned and gazed at her with his piercing eyes. "I'll see that you keep you word, Miss Adair—or that you pay for breaking it. Do you understand?"

He did not wait for an answer, but swiftly exited, leaving Sophia standing bewildered and alone in the room. Curious about what he had written, she walked hesitantly over to his desk.

*"Will depart at dusk Monday next with the objective of making*

*Woodsboro by midnight. Detachments will attack from the north and east, upon the preordained signal of each commanding officer. Troops are instructed to round up all known Tories, henceforth to be sent to the prison at Middletown. By His command and in His protection, and by His strength, not mine, may the gracious hand of Heaven preserve and keep us.*"

Sophia smiled to herself. Despite his reservations and to diminish her risk, he had made sure she would not be lying. She could tell the British that Colonel Grant Morgan was going to attack Woodsboro—she had even seen his orders with her own two eyes.

# CHAPTER 4

*Danger and deliverance make their advances together, and it is only the*
*last push that one or the other takes the lead.*
- Thomas Paine, The Crises

Sophia walked down the stairs with one hand on the bannister, her head held high despite the pounding of her pulse in her temples. Her trip back from the American post had been arduous and exhausting, a jolting, bone-rattling ride over uneven terrain and rutted roads. After sleeping a day and half on her return to the Spangler house, she had finally roused and prepared for the inquisition she accepted as inevitable.

"Miss Adair, how lovely to see you—and how relieved we are at your return."

Sophia beheld the concerned face of the British officer standing on the bottom stair, and the pounding in her temples began to resound in her throat. All she said was, "Major Briggs, you are here at an early hour," as she watched him bow low with elaborate and taunting courtesy.

"I stayed the night, Miss Adair. You cannot think I would leave—with you in such a condition after such an ordeal."

His words were deferential, but his eyes were not. They never were. Sophia felt her cheeks flush with anger, and then embarrassment, knowing the major would believe his advances caused the blush. She had disliked this man from the moment she'd met him, and not just because he was a British officer. Privilege and power—or the want of it—ruled his every move.

Even the reputation that followed him from his homeland was not one of which he should have been proud. Granted position, title, and authority by virtue of his birth, he had proved himself to be useless in camp and worthless on the field. So much so, that his superiors had sent him to America and made him an officer.

Sophia pushed these thoughts from her mind and tried to concentrate on the task at hand. "How kind of you, but it really wasn't necessary."

Briggs took two rapid steps toward her and, grabbing her hand in his, caressed her with his eyes. "Sophia, you appeared half dead when they brought you in."

"I was just tired," she responded with a tilt of her chin. "I do hope I no longer resemble the remark."

"Of course not, my dear," he said, bringing her hand to his lips and bowing. "You look as if no low-down dirty rebel Patriot ever crossed your path."

Sophia did not even attempt to smile. His constant condescending politeness and underhanded remarks about the Americans served only to sicken her, and make her long for the ruggedness of the patriot encampment.

It was no secret to her that Briggs was jealous of Colonel Morgan's reputation and competence as a soldier.

Contending at all times with a force superior to his own in numbers, arms, and equipment, the American officer routinely baffled the British in their attempts to subdue him. Briggs could do nothing but downplay the significance of the patriot's successes because he had nothing to show but a substantial trail of defeats.

Briggs must have noticed the look of revulsion and disdain. "Why is it that you trifle with my affections and have so little regard for my feelings, my dear?" He leaned even closer to whisper the words. "You know how deeply I care for you, Sophia."

Although mortified by the remark, Sophia was too well bred to show it. She knew this was just the beginning of a long and demanding ordeal, and so she smiled sympathetically, while offering no words of compassion or encouragement.

The British thought of her as young, carefree and frivolous, incapable of undergoing privations because she was so accustomed to luxury. She had to keep them thinking that she was fond of their admiration and high society—that she scorned the poor pageantry of colonial rank and authority.

"It's very good to be home," is all she said in reply.

"I know it's early, but Colonel Tyndale is here as well." Briggs paused for a moment as if to gauge her reaction. "He wants to speak with you, of course."

Sophia grabbed the bannister a bit more tightly. Tyndale oversaw the troops in the region and possessed a reputation for ruthlessness. Yet, like most British, he easily assumed the appearance of a gentleman—disguising his cruel side the same way the smooth, shiny hilt of a dagger conceals the dangerous blade within.

"What's wrong, my dear? You look frightened."

Sophia swallowed hard and smiled reassuringly. "Not

frightened, just surprised. I knew he would wish to speak with me, but… so soon?"

"So *soon*? You are not aware of the tumult your absence caused? He rode here as soon as he heard, and refused to leave until you were safely returned."

*Until I am thoroughly questioned*. Sophia knew that Colonel Tyndale ruled like a tyrant. His men obeyed him out of fear and dread of reprisal—not out of respect or esteem.

Allowing Major Briggs to loop her arm through his, Sophia followed dutifully through the gallery and into a sunny parlor where Colonel Tyndale and three other officers sat relaxing and sipping tea. When they saw her, all scrambled to their feet and bowed.

"Miss Adair, how good it is to see you well." Colonel Tyndale placed his hands on her shoulders and drew her to him in a manner that clearly indicated he believed himself personally responsible for her return. "I trust the uncivilized Americans were not overly rough with you."

"They were as well behaved as they know how to be," she replied with an air of sophistication. "I pity the creatures, though. So ragtag and dirty."

"Sit, sit, and tell us about your ordeal." Tyndale gave her little chance to decline as he led her to a chair. "That is, if it's not too awful to recall. I do not wish to be the cause of unpleasant memories."

Sophia took the seat offered, but did not offer any comment one way or the other about dredging up memories or her desire to offer testimony. The colonel seemed a bit taken aback by her silence and leaned down to gaze straight into her eyes. "You do understand you possess information which is your duty to give, which you must give, and which you cannot escape from giving."

Sophia's heart of its own accord began to thunder in her ears. "This is a formal inquiry then?"

Major Briggs quickly came to her aid. "Of course it is not a formal inquisition, Sophia. The colonel merely wishes to find out anything which may be helpful to us."

Sophia took a small napkin from the table and dabbed her eyes. "It is hard to recall, yet I shall do it—for the King's sake. But after this interview, I beg of you, if you value the service, do not pain me with mention of it again."

"Of course, of course, my dear." Tyndale turned his gaze to the men around him and nodded.

"Let's start at the beginning," he said as he handed Sophia a saucer of tea. "Your servant, Mash, told us a little. That you were out for a ride and the Patriots swept down upon you, insisting that you accompany them—something about you being a spy?"

"Yes, can you imagine anything so absurd? And then they blindfolded me and bound my hands." She held out one of her arms to show the red scratches from the rough hemp still visible. She'd taken the extra step of fighting hard enough that the Americans recognized the necessity of binding her.

"They bound you? A lady? Preposterous!"

She nodded and covered her eyes with her hands as if to blot out a painful vision.

"What then, dear?"

Sophia dabbed at her eyes dramatically and sniffled. "They took me to this officer—"

"What officer?" Major Briggs interrupted in an unusually loud voice.

Sophia paused as if searching her memory. "Colonel Maugen, I think it was."

"You must mean Colonel Morgan. Was it *he*? Are you sure?"

"Oh yes, that's it." She nodded. "Colonel Morgan." She pretended not to notice how they all leaned in just a little closer, and all seemed to inhale in unison, making it clear this was a man they both loathed and feared.

"He questioned me at length and then locked me up in this horrible room." She bent her head and squeezed her temples as if that would help rid herself of a terrible memory.

Colonel Tyndale stood and paced a moment before coming to a stop in front of her. "What did you think of Colonel Morgan?"

Sophia bit her lip to keep from blurting out that she thought him the most patriotic and courageous man she had ever laid eyes upon. "If you're asking how he treated me," she said, looking up innocently, "I would say no hostility was shown… but then again, little courtesy."

"No, that's not what I mean!" Tyndale boomed. "Did he seem in control of his men? Is he respected in the ranks? Was his camp fully fortified?" His voice began to soften. "We've heard he is in complete disarray."

When Sophia hesitated once again, Major Briggs stepped to her side. "Now, now dear. It's unfortunate that a lady of your standing had to come in contact with such animals, but it is important if you can remember anything."

Sophia wondered why Briggs seemed unable to express anything but anger, hatred and disdain when speaking of the Americans.

"I was really in no condition to note particulars," she said slowly, as if searching her memory, "but a dirtier and more forlorn establishment would be difficult to imagine." She paused, trying to find a way to describe the Americans in such a way as to enforce the British officers' inaccurate impression of their enemy. "As for Colonel Morgan, he appeared deficient in everything save self-esteem. Of course, as for his military prowess, I do not have the knowledge to comment."

While some of the men in the room laughed, Sophia's eyes drifted over to Major Briggs who stood warming his hands by the fireplace. She had never met a man so sensitive to cold. She studied him intently as he began to turn around to speak. The only thing he seemed to favor more than warmth was food, she thought to herself, as she gazed critically at his ample contour.

"But what of their soldiery. Did you chance to see any of them?" he asked.

"Oh, the soldiers." She shivered. "They appeared in terrible disarray—not like our soldiers here at all."

"Whatever do you mean?"

"Their uniforms, if you can call them such, were dirty and of no standard issue." She paused a moment for effect. "I cannot pretend to be knowledgeable about such things, but they did not seem to be familiar with military drill or the conduct of gentlemen." She heard a catch in her voice, and hoped the British would not grasp that it was caused by her deception.

Contrary to her words, all the men in the American camp had treated her with some level of courtesy, and she knew that even when not in the presence of the enemy, they were being drilled and prepared to encounter them. She cleared her throat. "They seem adept, though, at clinging to every straw that affords hope to their desperate cause."

"It is just as I thought," Briggs said, his voice tinged with disdain. "The cowards are incapable of fighting in the open. That is why they fight like Indians from the edges of the swamps."

"Appearances would warrant that conclusion," Sophia said, though she could barely suppress the contempt from her voice. Due solely to his lineage, Major Briggs considered himself a soldier and an infallible divinity—when in reality he was merely a bladder of emptiness and pride She studied his self-righteous expression as she calmly sipped her tea.

"What else? Do you remember anything else?"

"Oh, yes, now that you mention it," she said demurely, "Colonel Morgan asked me to convey a message to you."

"He did?" Again all the officers leaned forward so as not to miss a word.

"Yes. He asked me to warn you that you should leave this territory immediately or risk complete annihilation."

The men laughed in unison, save one, an older, wise-looking man, who met her gaze with an expression as alert as an imperious hawk. He tried to warn his fellow soldiers. "If we believe Morgan is just another rebel, just another bumbling military officer," he said, looking around the room, "we will lose a lot of blood."

Major Briggs waved his hand and laughed. "No military establishment can be expected to give serious attention to threats made from such an outrageous assembly of criminals. They should be reproached for fighting like savages, not feared."

Sophia smiled. "Indeed." Then she grew silent and thoughtful, causing the men to stop talking and look in her direction once again.

"Did you think of something else, Miss Adair?"

Sophia took a long sip of tea as if pondering something. "Perhaps… I mean, I saw something, but I do not know if it is anything worth noting."

"What is it, my dear?" Colonel Tyndale sounded unconcerned as he walked over to the fireplace and joined Briggs in warming his hands.

"Well, the camp seemed to be in a state of tremendous activity," she said. "I thought it odd, so when Colonel Morgan left the room to find some guards, I …"

Colonel Tyndale turned around and cocked his head. "Yes?"

"When he left the room to find some guards," she repeated, talking slowly, "I took the liberty of looking at a piece of paper on his desk." She paused, letting her gaze roam, one by one, to each man in the room. "I know it was wrong of me, but I …"

"No, no, no, my dear," Colonel Tyndale said as he hurried to her side. "You mustn't worry about that. Now what did you see?"

Sophia swallowed hard. "I saw a piece of paper…"

"Go on!" Tyndale thundered. "What did it say?"

"I tried to memorize it." Sophia closed her eyes for added effect as she repeated the words she had seen on the paper. When she had finished, utter silence filled the room. Nothing could be heard but the crackling of the fire and the steady, heavy breathing of the men surrounding her.

Sophia found herself holding her breath during the fateful moments. The tides of war hung in the balance—or at least the possible doom or success of her hurriedly conceived plan did.

"Do you think it's important?" Sophia gazed up at Tyndale with the most innocent expression she could muster.

The officers looked at one another, their eyes bright with excitement. "A fortnight, you say?" Tyndale turned away so she could not see his face. "Interesting. I suppose we shall prepare to send a greeting party, eh Briggs?"

"Indeed," Briggs replied. "We must draw every soldier we can get our hands on so we can end this nonsense once and for all."

Sophia's heart pounded as the trap fell into place. The plot had been launched noiselessly and without observation, just as calculated. The British would send everything they had to Woodsboro, while the majority of Morgan's men would be moving around their flank to capture Gladstone and confiscate needed supplies. If he kept his end of the deal, Morgan's own men would not be told the object of their expedition until the very last minute.

As the men whispered around her, Sophia took a deep breath and stared with a strange fascination at the room that had once seemed so familiar. Her uncle fulfilled every desire of her aunt and cousin, as was obvious from the room's decor. To enter his home was to enter a realm of lavishness and luxury, but it all seemed foreign to her now. After seeing how the patriots lived, this room exuded only extravagance, opulence, wealth, and waste.

Sophia wore a smiling mask upon a radiant face of calm as she stood and looked demurely around the room. "I have bestowed upon you what little information I possess. Is the interview complete?"

"Oh yes, my dear. Quite," Colonel Tyndale said, winking at his men. "I believe we've kept you long enough."

Major Briggs strode to her side and placed his lips purposefully and sensationally on her cheek. "The Crown will soon hear of a great victory thanks to you," he whispered breathlessly in her ear. "You shall be remembered a long time for this."

Sophia's heart skipped only one beat as she thought of the inevitable defeat that would soon commence due to her actions. *It may be better if they don't remember.* Before she had time to think another thought, she was swept out of the room with a wave of jubilant British officers busy preparing for their own demise.

# CHAPTER 5

*The boisterous sea of liberty is never without a wave.*
*- THOMAS JEFFERSON*

*Four weeks later*

The house seemed eerily quiet and empty as Sophia sat near the fireplace, enjoying the warmth and the soothing sense of isolation the silence brought. Until the previous evening, the home had been the scene of intense commotion as British officers arrived to attend private councils of war in the Spangler's library. Most had left by sundown, but couriers continued riding in and out until this morning when the last of the troops had departed.

They were all gone.

Sophia tried to remember a time when America was not one vast military camp, and regretted how she had taken that life—once so peaceful and calm—for granted. Living in the Spangler house had become like a prison, forcing her to balance the weight of dangerous responsibility with dreary, dismal days. It was hard to remember a time when nothing more troublesome than a mosquito crossed her path. Now she had to endure the constant pretentiousness and pomposity of men in red coats, and live with the knowledge that a war of epic proportions continued to expand.

As the logs spit and flamed, Sophia thought about the two days she had spent with the patriots. It was hard for her to believe two months had passed since the raid on the store-houses in Gladstone—especially since the resulting tumult had only recently subsided. According to what she'd over-heard, the British had been caught by surprise, losing not only valuable arms, ammunition, food, and horses—but something much more important—their pride.

After the escapade, they had questioned Sophia again about the dispatch she had seen, and she had repeated the message word for word. It was evident throughout the inter-rogation that they believed Colonel Morgan had led them into a trap, using her to set it. It apparently never occurred to them that she had been the one to devise the trap in the first place.

As for getting any details about the defeat directly, Sophia had not been successful. Tyndale's losses in the engagement were not confessed, nor would they probably ever be discov-ered. He allowed no one to discuss the topic, making it even more apparent that being outwitted by a rebel commander and his volunteer militia constituted a significant blow. The shadow of fear and intimidation Colonel Morgan cast over the British had grown markedly.

But now Sophia feared again for the rebels' safety. The British had reacted to their defeat by sending for reinforce-ments—and those reinforcements were close at hand. The increase in activity around the house proved that what they were planning was substantial, yet she had no means of conveying what she had learned to the Americans.

Sophia watched a log collapse in a shower of sparks, as her mind wandered to Colonel Morgan. Where was he now? Did he know the British were massing? She picked up the needlework on her lap, and put it down, trying without much success to keep her mind agreeably engaged. Perhaps she should go for a walk—or better yet, a ride.

The endless minutes of another endless day within the four walls of this room would serve to unnerve her if she did not find something to occupy her time. Just this morning she had heard that a ship carrying the additional troops had landed, and they were preparing for their march inland. She could barely stand to sit and think about what it meant for the Americans—or the fact that she had no way to deliver the news to them.

"Sophia, whatever are you doing just staring into the fire?"

Sophia jumped when her cousin Mary spoke and wondered how long she had been standing in the room.

"I declare, you've not been yourself ever since you were taken by those rebels!"

Sophia took up her needlepoint with imaginary calmness, and began working again, smiling at her cousin's comment. "I don't know what you mean. I'm fine."

Mary, who was more like a sister than a cousin, collapsed in the chair beside her with little ceremony. "Fine? You've barely talked since you got back. You sit in here and stare into space—just like you were doing when I came in just now."

Sophia forced a laugh and tried to act nonchalantly. "I did not know that was a crime."

Mary leaned in closer. "It's not, but it makes me wonder."

Sophia put her sewing down on her lap and cocked her head toward her cousin. "Wonder what?"

"What he was like."

Sophia returned her gaze to the fireplace as she felt heat begin to rise in her cheeks. She hoped Mary would think her nearness to the blaze caused the sudden surge. "What was who like?"

"Colonel Morgan, of course." Mary seemed unable to control her excitement. "Is it true what they say?"

"I don't know who 'they' are," Sophia said, bending over her stitches again, and pretending to concentrate. "So, I don't know what they say."

"*Everyone*, of course." Mary's voice seemed to rise an octave before she took a deep breath of exasperation. "What they say is that he is a master of disguise—like Proteus, he is able to change his shape at will." Mary stopped and leaned toward her. "And that beneath it all he is incredibly handsome."

Sophia laughed. "I'm surprised at you, Mary Spangler. How have you heard such things about an American officer, pray?" She tried to appear unaffected by the remark. "On my life, I've never heard that he is a master of disguise."

"He *is* handsome then? You thought so? You did not deny it!"

Sophia squinted as she tried to concentrate on the stitches. "No, I did not deny it. I suppose one could say he is a handsome man."

"*Incredibly* so?" Mary leaned toward her.

Sophia, exhaled loudly. "That is a very subjective thing. What may be handsome to you may not be to someone else."

Mary crossed her arms and pouted. "You're talking about Major Briggs now, aren't you? I can't understand why you don't like him. He is a very handsome man."

"Perhaps to you."

"Well, you must admit that he is not as objectionable as some who have sought your favor."

Sophia laughed loudly at the comment. "Not being as objectionable as others is hardly a reason to accept a man's hand in marriage."

"Well, I don't know why you won't consider it," Mary said. "He is an officer. Rumor has it he will soon be promoted."

Sophia grimaced. "Being an officer does not make a person worth marrying." She laid her sewing project on her lap and tried to change the subject. "What's this nonsense about Colonel Morgan being a master of disguise?" Although she knew her cousin had a penchant for exaggeration, she wanted to see what Mary had heard.

Mary stood and warmed her hands by the fire. "Oh, everyone talks of it. That he is able to disguise himself and walk into the British camps. That is how he knows where they are going to be and is able to defeat them." She paused a moment as if reflecting on something she had overheard. "He did it just last month they say."

Sophia smiled to herself. So that is how they are explaining their loss.

Mary walked over the piano, played a few bars and then sighed. "It's so quiet here today. I can hardly stand it."

Sophia laughed. "It's wonderfully quiet…and peaceful."

Mary's gaze darted over to her, as if she had said something irrational. "You don't *miss* them?"

Sophia didn't want to tell her much she despised them, yet didn't want to lie, and so she changed the subject. "Let's take a ride to Smithtown."

Mary wrapped her arms around herself and moved back toward the fire. "It's too cold."

"No it's not." Sophia got up, walked to the window, and

opened the drapes, allowing in a bountiful supply of sunbeams. "It's a beautiful day!"

"I know the sun is shining, but that doesn't mean it is warm outside." Mary shivered again in an exaggerated way.

"Come on, Mary. You can't stay penned up pining away over the departure of the British forever."

"I'm not pining away," Mary said, defending herself. "I just miss them."

"Well, if you take a ride with me to Smithtown, you'll forget all about them. I'm sure of it."

Sophia studied her cousin's reaction as she considered the idea. Although the two had practically grown up together and were once very close—they were now as opposite as could be. Her uncle had tried to instill in both of them the necessity of acting at all times the part of a lady, but the trait had come somewhat more easily to Mary than to Sophia. Mary relished entertaining and mingling within the circles of sophisticated society that her father's business required, but she was neglectful of responsibility and careless about her obligations.

Sophia, on the other hand, preferred solitary meanderings as opposed to the loud gatherings that Mary so enjoyed. Being trapped in the middle of a war, there was as much of one as there was little of the other, so the two were forever at odds.

"You're right, I suppose," Mary finally said. "I should get out for some fresh air, but I'm not sure I feel like riding that far."

"That far?" Sophia laughed. "It's only six miles for heaven's sake."

As she waited for Mary to make up her mind, Sophia walked over the window. Smithtown was not a town at all, but a few buildings clustered together—one of which was a tavern. Country folk would often stop there on their way to

Charles Town to get their news—or their gossip—whatever the case might be. Mary and Sophia did not venture into the tavern, but an open field nearby provided a place to picnic and a location to meet with friends or those who were just passing through.

"I'll have Mash saddle Donovan and Spirit right away." Sophia decided to take Mary's hesitation in not saying no, as a definite yes, and hurried from the room before Mary could change her mind.

It didn't take long for their horses to be saddled, and Mary and Sophia, along with Mash as an escort, went cantering down the sandy road. Sophia found it invigorating to feel the strength of her gelding beneath her and the breeze on her face as they let the horses pick up the pace.

Although this was the bleakest time of year, it yet held much promise. The dogwoods and redbuds, still tight asleep, would soon be reborn by the sun to soften and assuage the landscape. Even without the vivid colors of spring, the scenery seemed to be spun of gold by some heavenly hands, so that not even the thought of a raging war could make the day unpleasant. With her fingers on the reins and the sun on her back, dismal thoughts disappeared, melting away like dewdrops at dawn.

At the speed they traveled, it seemed like only minutes before they were in sight of the small crossroads. As usual, the area was teeming with travelers stopping by the tavern, and others just standing around and talking. Mary soon found someone she knew and reined her horse to a stop, while Sophia rode a few steps farther taking in the sights and listening to the low hum of conversation around her.

She urged her horse toward a grassy area, and dismounted, allowing him to graze a few minutes. Everyone around her seemed in a gay mood, laughing, talking, catching up on the news, or just taking a rest from a long journey on a sunny winter's day.

After a few moments of watching the activity around her, Sophia's gaze fell upon a man selling hides, furs, and assorted trinkets from the back of his wagon. His shirt-sleeves were rolled up to his elbows, showing off brown arms that were brawny and strong. A hint of a memory caused her gaze to travel casually to his face, and the spark suddenly crystallized into explosive recognition.

Although he wore a scraggly beard and floppy hat that denoted a lowly trader, his brilliant eyes were unmistakable. Sophia jerked her horse from his meal and began to walk toward him. "Sophia, where are you going?" Mary rode toward her, and hastily dismounted as she struggled to keep up.

"Look at these wonderful ribbons!" Sophia answered. "I must have one."

Colonel Morgan paid no attention to her, but continued to hold up furs to display to the people who passed by.

"I'd like one of your ribbons, sir."

His dark, stormy eyes shot her a look of impatient tolerance that almost caused her to turn away, but at last he answered. "Which one, lassie?"

"The blue one, if I may."

Morgan turned toward the wagon and selected the ribbon. A halfpenny, miss," he said in an irritated voice, regarding her now with cold and calculating eyes.

Sophia reached into her pocket and pulled out the requested payment. When he held out his hand, she intentionally missed his upturned palm and the coin fell to the ground.

"Oh, dear how clumsy of me." She bent down to retrieve the coin, while the colonel did the same.

"Three regiments arriving within a day and more within the week to Shay's Corner," she whispered.

He picked up the coin and stood. "No harm done, miss." He tipped his hat, and turned his back as if he had not heard a word she'd said.

# CHAPTER 6

*All might be free if they valued freedom, and defended it as they should.*
\- SAMUEL ADAMS

olonel Morgan sat in the shadows, straining his ears for any sound other than his own men and horses as they moved. He flinched at each groan and creak of the wheels, but knew he had time on his side. The British, marching in the dark, would be slow in their progress—and traveling in unfamiliar territory would subject them to delay.

At the edge of some woods that lined the road, Morgan halted his command. He told his men where to position two small guns, and watched as they moved them this way and that to get just the right angle. The field pieces were a result of the raid a month ago when the British had abandoned their warehouses with the objective of annihilating Morgan and his men. He smiled at the brilliance of the plan and how smoothly it had been implemented, then frowned when he thought of Sophia Adair and the danger she had placed herself in to communicate with him.

When one of the soldiers signaled to him that the guns were in place, he began to relax. The men had marched all night to get here, and it was now almost dawn. There had been very little talking and no complaining throughout the journey—only the shuffling tramp of feet, the steady rumbling of wheels, and the creak, rattle, and clank of harness and accouterment.

This group of men had already proved that they possessed unparalleled courage. They'd resisted the British without any provisions other than what they provided themselves, and they continued their resistance even though there was little hope of reward.

Yes, the hands that held the musket sometimes appeared awkward, but they were steady. The men might not be able to maneuver in the open as the British did, but they could fight. When one of them fell, another would step promptly forward to take his place *and* his gun if necessary. These men were dauntless, but not reckless; they were confident, but not careless. No one knew what the day would bring forth, but none appeared overly concerned about the outcome.

The foe Morgan and his men faced in this section of the country was twofold—the British regulars who had to be dealt with head on, and the insidious, malicious Loyalists who often lurked in the shadows, inflicting misery and anguish at every turn.

These two forces occupied all the strong positions in South Carolina and were well-supplied with arms, ammunition and military equipment of every kind. The Patriots, on the other hand, had no place to resort for safety except the swamps, and no supplies of any kind except what was taken from their own scanty stock.

As the war lingered on, the patriots' own homes had

become the most dangerous place to be, as their Loyalist neighbors, wishing to benefit from the wealth flowing from the Crown, would inform the British of their locations. Morgan had therefore adopted a tactic that combined secrecy and stealth, speed and surprise, and he knew how and when to use all four better than any other officer in the field. Seldom lingering in one spot, he changed ground with Indian-like policy, baffling the British efforts to rein him in.

With preparations complete, Morgan relaxed a little in his saddle, but he remained keenly aware they needed a victory today. Distress and disease were now reaping a far richer death harvest than the British had been capable of bestowing. The supplies of war and sustenance for his men would go a long way to improving health and morale, and intensifying their trust and confidence.

With a signal from Morgan, the soldiers dropped where they stood and were instantly asleep without so much as unrolling a blanket. Worn out by fatigue, these men would still be ready to fight after some much-needed repose. Despite their deficiencies in arms, they were capable of suffering more, daring more, and achieving more than just about any other group similarly organized.

Morgan dismounted and sat down beneath a tree, using its strong trunk to rest his weary back. He was tired, but did not feel inclined to sleep. Instead, he gazed at the men resting peacefully around him and tried to envision the best way to face the approaching enemy. Only by surprise could he hope to be successful—and he was relying on *that* as his main offense.

Just as he had done with the last mission, Morgan kept the destination of this operation quiet from all of his men, not providing the vaguest notion concerning his purpose. He had even detailed a small party to another area to divert the attention of the enemy—or any informant.

He didn't want to take any chances that someone from his own quarters could interfere or warn the British that he knew Tyndale was being reinforced.

But a whisper of unease bothered him. If he attacked now, would he be putting Sophia Adair in danger? Certainly the arrival of fresh troops was known only to a few. It would not be hard for the British to look around and discover who had tipped him off. The thought had made him restless from the beginning and still kept him so.

As his body started to relax, he drifted off to a fretful sleep, and was brought back to consciousness by the low, distant sound of creaking leather and clattering chains. As he began to wake his men, the steady hum turned into the distinct sound of hooves hitting stones and rocks, of wheels turning. He looked toward the horizon and saw the first slight glimmerings of dawn. Even with the benefit of light, the British would be tired from their journey, and the low haze clinging to the ground would help to hide the number of men attacking.

Morgan motioned for his men to fan out, and watched them skirt the main highway, keeping to the deep shadows. The first wave of the attack would involve some of his best sharpshooters, who would need no instruction from him. They would form behind every tree, bush, and rock, find a target, and fire. If the enemy made a rush toward the spot, there would be no one there, but there would be another nearby to take his place. Although attacking three times their numbers, the patriots would be assisted by the surprise of the operation and the ability to deceive.

Morgan tried to radiate confidence and strength as he ordered his men into position. He was everywhere at once, dashing up and down, imbuing them with enthusiasm and courage. The thought of procuring sustenance for his men and horses while inflicting deadly force upon the enemy now controlled his entire mind.

The men followed his commands with no reluctance or doubt. Isolated as they were, any indecision on his part, any mischance, any wavering or hesitancy—and the entire regiment would be lost.

It seemed like only minutes later that the enemy came lumbering into view, looking gigantic as they filled the road and the space on each side. With his eyes on the target and all his senses alert and vigilant, Morgan counted and calculated their strength. Three regiments she had said, yet they seemed to keep coming. He hesitated for a moment, fearing a trap. Could he trust her? *Should* he trust her? It would be just like the British to send a beautiful woman across the lines to entrap the Americans. Had he fallen for it too easily?

Pondering his dilemma, he allowed his eyes to roam down the road and his spirits started to rise. Trick or not, these troops and horses appeared tired from their journey, their bodies slumped and sagging—and he could see no escort. Was it foolishness or arrogance that led them to march without preparation into a land occupied by the enemy? Morgan smiled grimly. Whichever the case, it was an attack impossible to pass by.

"Quite a coincidence running into reinforcements like this, eh, Colonel?"

Grant glanced back at Captain Tate who had ridden up behind him.

"Yes. And a lucky one at that."

"We going to attack?"

Morgan nodded. "Don't see why not. It appears the enemy is within our reach, and certainly within our power to defeat."

"Could be more dragoons over there." Tate nodded toward the river.

"Can't waste my time worrying about what might be over there," Morgan turned in his saddle and motioned for another officer. He rode a little closer, running his gaze over the road a moment, and then swiftly gave his orders. He had taken in the whole situation in one rapid glance, and, at once, made his final dispositions.

"Take your men around to the back." He pointed to a scuff of trees. "Stick to the shadows over there."

The sergeant nodded and saluted, then rode away.

"You can attack from the front with me," Morgan said. "Rooney and Johns are covering the flanks."

Tate nodded as he sat watching the column of British move slowly through the shadows of early dawn with a contemplative look upon his face.

When the signal was given, the attack came with an abruptness for which the enemy was unprepared, and with an adeptness they were not expecting. Morgan's men struck swiftly, suddenly and remorselessly, sending the British scurrying into defensive positions. Many of the Redcoats had heard of the effectiveness of the militia's guns and did not care to face them, so they scrambled for their lives through the thick bramble and brush.

This, coupled with the ferocity with which Morgan's men swept down upon these seasoned fighters, forced even the veteran soldiers to flee in panic. The terror in their ranks spread like wildfire, making their departure in no way a quiet and orderly retirement, but a retreat conducted in dire confusion and fright.

Although greatly outnumbered, Morgan's men continued firing from behind the hedges and the rocks, coolly reloading their guns, moving to another spot, and firing again. The British had long ago learned that it was useless to search out these ghostly forms. Each shooter would appear for a moment, fire, and then melt away, only to be replaced by another in a different location with fatal shot. Like swift shadows, the patriots would speed through the dusky forest, reloading as they ran, and join the fight again.

In just a few minutes time, it became a matter of enraged surprise on one side, and wondering exultation on the other. Who could have foretold that the small militia could once again turn the tide and defeat the powerful and well-equipped British army with such unexpected results?

When it was over, Morgan sat on his horse beneath a mass of trees and took a deep breath of relief. In addition to the prisoners, he would once again be restocked with firearms, horses, ammunition and supplies. He bowed his head and said a quick prayer of thanks before his thoughts turned to Sophia Adair. Her act of bravery may have just saved this entire region—though no one but he would ever know it.

"Pretty nice piece of work for one day, I'd say. Congratulations, Colonel." Captain Tate leaned forward on his saddle staring at the bounty. "How'd you know about it?"

Morgan turned his head slowly and studied the soldier intently. "Know about what?"

"These reinforcements." His laugh sounded forced. "You can't think I'd believe you just happened upon it."

In prior days Morgan would have perhaps shared the information with his good friend, but the concerns of Sophia Adair stopped him. He stared at the captain with a look that made the younger man flinch. "Thank you. That message was well conveyed earlier."

Morgan squeezed his gelding's sides and rode toward some of his men going through crates in a wagon. "Take what we need and destroy what we cannot carry," he ordered, before turning his horse to ride to the front of the line.

# CHAPTER 7

*The Sun never shined on a cause of greater worth*
- THOMAS PAINE, COMMON SENSE

olonel Morgan sat on the wide windowsill staring out at the brilliant display created by the setting sun. His mind, however, remained focused on decisions of war rather than on the magnificent array of colors before him. The sound of footsteps, followed by the door creaking open, interrupted his quiet musings. Turning to glance over his shoulder, he watched Captain Tate stomp his feet a few times on an old throw rug and toss his hat on a chair.

"I guess you heard the Redcoats are pretty bloody upset about that attack Monday last," Tate said.

Morgan stood and shrugged his shoulders, then turned back to the view out the window with his hands on his hips. "Perhaps they will take the hint and leave us alone."

"I wouldn't count on that." Tate slumped into one of the chairs and propped his muddy boots on the edge of the desk.

"I think it's making them more spiteful and unpleasant." He glanced over his shoulder toward Morgan. "If that's possible, I mean."

"Truly?" Morgan began to get an uneasy feeling about his friend's visit. "I had hoped the schooling I've already provided would be enough to teach Colonel Tyndale that he has altogether mistaken the character of the men he is dealing with." He gazed back at Tate. "If he renders another lesson necessary, you can rest assured I will be happy to enlighten him.

"Oh, I think he's looking for something other than another fight," Tate answered absently while rubbing a piece of dirt off the sleeve of his coat.

Morgan walked casually back to his desk, sat, and picked up a quill to begin some correspondence. "How do you mean?" He pretended not to be interested in the conversation, but had a strange feeling that something was amiss.

"Word in Smithtown has it that he's questioning everyone at the Spangler house. He seems to think he has an informant close to him."

Even as the calm, low-toned voice said the words, realization of what they revealed became a black abyss yawning before Morgan. His heart jerked and rolled over in his chest, then plummeted into his boots—leaving him breathless. He casually put the quill down, fearing Tate would see how unsteady his hand had become. A low roar commenced in his ears, making it hard to speak, or even think.

"The Spangler house you say? Whatever for?"

Tate snickered and stood. "Come on, Grant. We both know—and I suppose the Brits do too—that it's not just luck that puts them right under your nose time and again."

Morgan laughed and hoped it didn't sound too forced. "Of course, it's not just luck. It's good soldiering."

Tate frowned and then grew silent and meditative for a

moment. "I wonder if it somehow has something to do with that woman."

Morgan walked back to the window and leaned his shoulder into the wooden frame, searching his mind and wondering if ever by word, conduct, or deed he had hinted that Sophia Adair was his informant in front of this man. "What woman is that?" he asked as if he had forgotten the whole affair.

"The one you brought here. The supposed spy. Remember?"

"Surely you jest." Morgan looked at Tate over his shoulder. "I got the distinct impression she didn't like us very much."

Tate laughed. "Well, if you want a bad opinion of yourself, ask a woman for it. That's for sure." He paused and rubbed his chin. "She seemed a bit hostile to me too, but one can never tell with beauties such as that." He looked back up at Morgan and studied him. "No doubt you would tell me if she were on our side."

"As far as beauty, I remember nothing of her looks." Although he could feel his temple pulsing with the suppression of emotion, Morgan stared into his friend's eyes with unwavering resolve. "I saw a Tory and nothing more." He walked to the fireplace and put his hands down to warm them. "Anyway, I should think questioning those in the Spangler house would be a waste of time for them. Everyone knows the residents there are devoted to the Crown."

"So it is assumed, but they've been soundly licked twice. I presume they believe the third time is proverbial and the odds must turn." He glanced toward Morgan, but did not linger on him. "If it's not someone there, then it would have to be one of their own," he said musingly.

"Yes, well such things *do* occur." Morgan turned and crossed his arms, staring accusingly at his captain.

Tate didn't notice—or at least pretended not to notice—the accusation. He slid his feet off the desk and stood to leave. "Anyway, I came to report that the men are going to drill with the new arms this afternoon in the lower meadow."

"Very well."

Morgan listened to the door close, and let out his breath. Had he deceived her somehow? Had he acted too interested in the Spangler house? Too unconcerned? Perhaps a female's intuition had indeed been better than his own.

His concern soon turned to anger and he pounded the mantel with his fist. Lands, he knew they'd start retracing their steps. They'd been licked cleanly twice in a month's time by a small contingency of militia. Of course, they knew someone was helping him! And yet he'd allowed her to fight alone, unaided and unsupported in one great silent, never-ending conflict of wit, will and cunning.

Colonel Morgan decided he had to act and do so without delay. He had already allowed this to go too far, and regretted permitting it at all. Her dangerous conduct had to stop, and he was the only one with the knowledge and authority to compel her to do so.

Sophia had arisen at an early hour, while the dew was still wet and the sun barely a hint on the horizon, but had not yet brought herself to leave her room. The house was once again full of British officers and she dreaded the thought of pretending she enjoyed their company.

The days had passed fleetingly since her visit with the patriots, and her sentiments had alternated between exaltation and despair as news from the field revealed a great victory one day and a terrible defeat the next. Sophia took solace in the fact that whatever the British gained in ground from the patriots, they paid for so dearly in numbers.

As for Colonel Morgan and his militia, she had heard they were constantly on the move, offering battle one day and eluding one the next. Colonel Tyndale's desperation to destroy this homegrown army grew more determined each day.

Over the last few weeks, Sophia had become restless and impatient too, wanting more than anything for the war to end, even as the turmoil seemed to escalate around her. Agitated this morning that she couldn't do more to bring about her desired result, she tried without success to think of something pleasant. She soon gave up on that endeavor, and concentrated instead on getting her unruly locks to cooperate.

After trying a number of different styles and being enthused about none of them, Sophia rested her chin on her hands, and stared musingly into the mirror. She had aged since this war had begun. She could see it in the small lines and creases that now edged her mouth and eyes. Concern, worry, and the weight of responsibility—all commingled in her serious stare. She tried to smile, to lighten the look, but it appeared more like a grimace, so she turned away and stood.

Just as she did so, the sound of voices floated in to her, along with playful barking of the Spangler's young dog. Although not exceptionally loud, something about the tone of the voices made her go to the window. Scanning the landscape for a moment and seeing nothing, she was just about to turn around when she noticed some movement near the gate.

Her heart leaped into her throat as she watched Colonel Morgan stride into view, calm and unruffled, gesturing with his hands as he talked to two British soldiers. Although dressed again as a lowly trader, he appeared the very picture of a soldier.

Sophia grabbed the windowsill for support when she noticed two more British officers walk toward him. Morgan appeared relaxed and smiling as he nodded his head in reply to their questions, but his answers apparently did not satisfy them. They pointed toward the house and he obediently followed.

Even though Sophia could not quite make out the words, she guessed the import of the situation. She knew Colonel Tyndale was in the library, and feared Morgan was being taken to him for further questioning—perhaps had been officially summoned to appear here. They had already questioned her and everyone in the household, making it obvious that they suspected—or *knew*—something.

Trying to appear calm, Sophia started down the stairs, though she had to hold onto the handrail to steady her shaking legs. *What could he possibly be doing so near? Could there be trouble he is trying to warn me about?*

"Is something wrong, Miss Adair?"

Major Briggs stood at the bottom of the stairs, his brows drawn close as he studied her with slit-eyed intensity.

"No, nothing is wrong." She laughed. "But I believe someone came in that I must talk to."

"Talk to, Miss Adair?"

Pushing passed him without another word, Sophia proceeded to the library, where she heard the low murmuring of voices. Opening the door without knocking, she stepped in with a boldness that surprised even her. All heads turned expectantly to the door as it opened and she found herself the object of five sets of probing eyes.

"Oh," she said meekly. "I fear I've interrupted."

Colonel Tyndale waved his hand graciously. "A welcome distraction I assure you." His voice sounded smooth and friendly, and he possessed a smile of imperial casualness, but she knew all were masks for his evil intentions. It mattered little if he appeared angry or joyful, if he spoke kindly or harsh. He was the ruler here. He reigned by force with little regard for who or what he destroyed in the process.

The air in the room was thick with tobacco smoke and smelled faintly of spirits, making Sophia instantly nauseous and light-headed. Yet knowing that the slightest mistake in look or tone could unmask her, she pushed away her fear and gazed around the room with a casual air.

In addition to Colonel Tyndale, she saw a soldier sitting at a desk, apparently taking notes about what was being said. Two other men, the sentries, she supposed, seemed to be conversing in low tones by the fireplace, and in front of the window stood Colonel Morgan.

She allowed her eyes to rest on him for only a moment, long enough to see that his expression was one of unconcern, at least an enemy might suppose. Yet beneath the half-lowered lids she noticed hidden signs of apprehension—though she had a feeling it was *her* safety that concerned him, not his own.

"Do you recognize this man, Miss Adair?" Tyndale's voice broke through the silence and Sophia's nerves.

"Why, of course." She turned to face Tyndale and looked at him with an unwavering gaze. "When you are finished with your business with him, I would like to have a word as well." She curtsied politely. "But please don't let me interrupt. I apologize for the intrusion."

She turned to leave, but Tyndale stepped in front of her.

"What do you mean you'd like to have a word with him, pray? This is not a man I would think a niece of Charles Spangler would be familiar." His tone had changed from gentle and jovial to harsh and testy.

The other men in the room stopped talking and seemed to pause, waiting for her reply.

Sophia stared up at Tyndale as if completely taken aback, although she tried to remain gracefully relaxed and poised. "Why, whatever do you mean? Why should I not be familiar with him?" She began to tap her foot on the floor as if impatient, but inside her courage began to falter.

The plan, she had so hurriedly devised, no longer appeared achievable or even logical. Sophia feared that her eyes or her voice, or both, would deceive her, yet she drew deep from within to appear unaffected. "Has he done something wrong?" She removed her gaze from Tyndale and scanned the faces of the other men, searching for answers.

All the men seemed confused and looked from Sophia to the stranger, while Colonel Morgan stood quietly with hat in hand by the window. She watched his eyes wander around the room, apprising each man, and saw the raw confidence on his face intensify. Seeing the calm features and penetrating eyes of a man who knew no fear gave her some faith and reassurance.

"He is here concerning military matters, which you would not understand," Tyndale said in response to her question. "It is only for questioning."

Sophia laughed loudly and gleefully at that. "Military matters? But he is simply a trader who sold me a piece of ribbon. What would he know of military matters?" Even as she said the words, a low roar commenced in her ears and Sophia began to have an overwhelming sense of doom.

She did not even know if Colonel Morgan was playing the part of a trader today. He could be pretending to be a completely different character for all she knew. Why, just a few weeks ago Mary had told her he was a master of disguise.

"Is that true?" Colonel Tyndale turned to Morgan.

"The evidence is in her hair," Morgan answered calmly. "I was just getting ready to explain all that to you."

Tyndale's eyes returned to Sophia. "Is that the ribbon?" He nodded toward the one she wore in her hair.

Sophia reached up and touched the thin slice of fabric, the color rising in her cheeks when she realized it adorned her hair. She wondered if Morgan would think her bold—or perhaps patently childish—for wearing it. All she could think of to say was, "It is one of my favorites."

She glanced again at Colonel Morgan, and tried to read what he was thinking—a useless endeavor. His eyes appeared to be a means to search other people's thoughts, not reveal his own.

"I don't understand why you are questioning this man." She turned back to Colonel Tyndale. "Has he done something wrong?"

"No one recognized him, and he's been lurking in the area," Tyndale said coldly. "You can vouch for his character?"

Sophia laughed lightly. "I did not say I can vouch for his character, sir. I can only say he is a trader with whom I've done honest business." She turned her attention back to Morgan. "And I was hoping I could purchase another ribbon. To match the one I have."

"Can't say as you can or can't as I don't know how long I'll be detained." He sounded terse, and although he appeared relaxed, the look on his face remained guarded and somewhat threatening.

The ensuing silence seemed dreadfully loud and sinister as Sophia waited nervously for Colonel Tyndale to respond. Yet she crossed her arms and tapped her foot, staring defiantly at the British officer to give the impression he was detaining the trader for a trifle when matters of great magnitude loomed. "May I presume that you have concluded your business with this man so that I may begin mine?" she asked at last.

"Are you trying to rush me, Miss Adair?" Tyndale's tone had menace in it—perceptible and distinct. Having spent so much time in his company, Sophia was familiar enough with his character to know that those who incited his anger were not disposed to rouse it again.

"Why, I wouldn't do such a thing for the wide, wide world, Colonel Tyndale," she replied with innocent astonishment. "I'll wait in the parlor to conduct my business with this gentleman. You can kindly send him to me when you have concluded yours."

She turned and walked out the door, wanting more than anything to stay, but knowing that if she did, she might appear a bit too anxious. It was just a ribbon after all, hardly a reason to get into a quarrel with the commanding officer of the British army.

Before heading to the parlor, Sophia made a hasty trip to her chamber for her sewing basket and a piece of paper. Her fingers began to tremble as she tried to hurry, and she fumbled miserably in her task of undoing some of the stitches of the ribbon.

Finally, her mission accomplished, she put the ribbon back in her hair, and flew down the stairs to the parlor. She began pacing its length, twisting her dress with her hands as she walked, wondering if she'd said too much or too little... acted too anxious or too indifferent. The steady ticking of the clock made the seconds feel like hours as she waited for the supposed trader to appear.

At last she heard footsteps and whirled around. Colonel Tyndale's aide appeared in the doorway first, closely followed by Colonel Morgan, who strode in as relaxed as if he were being received as a guest at tea. She found his calm bearing and dauntless resolution intimidating.

"The trader, miss," the aide said before retreating to the far side of the room to stir the smoky fire.

Sophia raised her eyes to look into Morgan's, expecting perhaps to read something there. But his dark countenance was as remote as ever, distant—if not perhaps a little angry. He suddenly seemed taller than she had remembered, more rugged, and not a little forbidding.

"I've got no ribbons with me, miss," he said somewhat harshly before she had time to ask the question. His face was grim, and the muscles at the corners of his lean jaw appeared knotted and hard.

"Oh, how very disappointing." Sophia stomped her foot like a spoiled child, causing the aide to glance over his shoulder before going back to his business. From his look of disgust, she assumed she had reinforced her reputation as one who demanded immediate service and thought her status lofty enough that she should receive it.

"Do you sell in Smithtown often?"

"Whenever it strikes me." Colonel Morgan's tone made it clear he wanted no part of meeting with her again. "I hold to no schedule."

"Oh dear." Sophia sniffled, as if not getting a matching band was as close to the end of the world as she could envision. "I did so want another for a special dinner next month." She wiped away an imaginary tear and looked up at him. "I don't suppose you could bring one here. I would pay extra."

"Look here, lassie." His tone was harsh and cold, making it clear he intended to leave little opportunity for dispute. "I sell furs, and sometimes trade for trinkets and ribbons. There's no way of tellin' if I got another like that one."

Sophia remained undeterred. She pulled the ribbon out

of her hair and handed it to him. "Well, here then. It will do me no good to have only one. Take this one and see if you have another. I'll pay double if you do."

Morgan reluctantly took the ribbon, a questioning look in his eyes that seemed to turn to vexation in an instant.

"If your business is finished here, I'll show you out." The aide, who had apparently been listening to the entire conversation, began to walk toward the door.

Morgan nodded his head as his eyes drilled into Sophia. "My business is done here."

Sophia took a step toward him and put her hand on his arm, blinking in surprise when she felt the solid muscle beneath his sleeve. "You will look for another just like that one, won't you?" She nodded toward the ribbon. "It's very *special* to me."

Morgan looked from the ribbon to her face, and started to remove her hand with a firm, powerful grasp. It appeared he would not tolerate another second's delay, yet he surprised her by pausing a moment, still clasping her hand in his strong hold. "I told you, miss. I got no more ribbons."

His touch felt as gentle as his voice sounded harsh, as if he were trying to communicate without words. Perhaps it was only her imagination. A moment later, he dropped her hand and stomped toward the door as if angry at the entire encounter.

Sophia turned her back and listened to his footsteps. She heard a short pause, as if he had turned to look at her, or perhaps had something else to say, but then the door clicked shut and his footsteps melted away. Sophia did not move, even as she heard voices floating in through the window, and then the sound of a horse trotting down the lane.

# CHAPTER 8

*An army of principles can penetrate where an army of soldiers cannot.*
- THOMAS PAINE

*Five days later*

olonel Morgan paced the length of his headquarters with the piece of blue ribbon in his hand, muttering under his breath. At last he sat and pounded its surface with a fist. "What were you thinking, Sophia Adair?"

He had known instantly the ribbon contained something significant, but why had she taken such a chance? The note he had discovered between the linings of the fabric had been comprised of just seven words, obviously hurriedly scribbled: *Supplies arriving by River Rd in morning.*

Morgan knew the road well and comprehended at once how easy it would be to ambush a supply train. Paralleled by sloping hills and forests, large numbers of troops could be easily blocked in a small area.

The advance notice was all he had needed to position his men in such a way that the wagons were cut off from reinforcements behind. He had not lost a man, and the resulting victory could justly be considered one of the most successful of the war.

But the hands holding the ribbon began to tremble when he thought about what would have happened if the British had caught her writing the note—or had checked the ribbon after she had given it to him. Her task had required calmness, courage, and resolve—but it had also required a recklessness that could have placed her neck in a noose. In doing what she regarded as her duty she seemed to have no fear—or sense.

Thoughts of Sophia Adair had crossed Morgan's mind often, but meeting her like that, face-to-face in the home where she resided, had enlightened him to traits in her character he had never suspected.

When with the British she acted like one who moves only in refined circles, all grace and sophistication. She gave the illusion she did not like to dwell on serious matters or concern herself with thoughts that did not involve her own gratification. Somehow she was able to mask her observant eyes, and she had even been able to demolish Colonel Tyndale's defenses with a mere smile.

Morgan understood now how completely fooled the British really were by her supposed loyalty and her lack of wit or will. She relied heavily on the importance of being underestimated—and she played the part well. Despite the tremendous obstacles she faced and the weight of responsibility, she showed no signs of slowing down or giving up.

Putting down the ribbon and standing, Morgan began to pace when he thought of the new danger she now faced. His scouts had reported that the British were pulling out of the region, moving closer to the coast where they could be more easily supplied. Staff officers, quartermasters and commissaries, together with clerks, aides and soldiers, were on the move with their baggage to the small coastal town of Duncannon.

Although Morgan knew that *he* would be credited with the sudden departure, one person and one person alone was responsible for their move.

Sophia Adair.

That alone would be good news, but this was war, and there could never be an action without a reaction. Now that the British were leaving or gone, families like the Spanglers—and others who had helped the British—were in great danger. There were those in the neighborhood, and even members of his own militia, making threats of violence against the Tories. It would be almost impossible for Morgan to stop a marauding band of Patriots or deserters from taking vengeance on those who had aided and abetted the enemy.

To further complicate matters, a contingency of Continentals had finally been sent down to help defend the region and were expected any day. Morgan would have no control over those soldiers, and he was the only person alive who knew that one member of the Spangler household was not only a Patriot, but was also the sole reason for his recent victories.

Morgan glanced out the window at the afternoon sun. Despite the danger, he had to go warn her of the growing peril and insist she leave. If he left now he could be there before nightfall.

Without hesitation he donned his old trader's coat in case he needed to act the part again. Throwing the ribbon in his pocket for good luck, he strode into the hallway and informed the sentry he'd return by daybreak, before exiting out the back door.

"Scouting alone again, Colonel?"

Morgan paused and glanced around at the soldier who stood on the porch right outside the door, casually leaning his shoulder into the side of the building. Morgan did not stop walking, but continued toward his horse. "Make sure the men are ready for the Continentals if they get here before I return, Captain Tate."

The gorgeous pageantry of the west was fading, making the silhouettes of the dark trees appear as sentinels of the night. Colonel Morgan tied his horse in a stand of pines and walked to the twin gateposts that marked the boundary of the Spangler property. The twilight air was mild, with a still-ness so profound he could hear the barking of a dog more than a mile away.

Morgan stayed in the shadows of the house, searching for any movement or sign that the British had left anyone behind. It was just about dark when he was drawn to the back of the stately home by the soft melodious sound of bubbling laughter.

Peering from behind a tree, he saw Sophia sitting on the ground, playing with a wolfhound pup. Her innocent playful-ness and mirth made him realize how very young she was, creating yet another contradiction to her character. Young yet wise, serious yet lighthearted, feminine yet bold—opposing traits that combined to create an intriguing allure. He could not recall ever having seen her smile so naturally, let alone laugh, and the sound of it triggered a stirring in his heart.

Remembering his duty, Morgan drew closer and whis-pered her name. She must have recognized his voice because for a moment she remained frozen in place as if she thought she had imagined that she'd heard a voice at all. Then she slowly turned her head and looked over her shoulder to meet his gaze.

"Are you alone?" he whispered.

Sophia did not speak, but raised one finger into the air as if asking him to wait. Clicking her fingers to call the dog, she walked into the house, and returned a few moments later with a wrap around her shoulders. Without acknowledging him or speaking, she turned toward a little-used trail that led deep into the garden.

Sophia walked down a series of paths to her favorite spot in the garden—a small, secluded clearing far from the house. Stopping by a fountain with a bench, she turned and watched Colonel Morgan advance cautiously from the shadows, his formidable figure exuding physical strength and power even in the darkness.

"We are alone now, I believe," she said when he reached her.

Morgan nodded and stood for a moment with his hands on his hips, his jaw set sternly as he stared at her. Then, without warning, he grabbed her by the shoulders and shook her.

"You little fool! What made you give me the message about the supply train?"

Sophia blinked in surprise. His voice had trembled ever so slightly, as had his hands, but his blue-gray eyes burned into hers with a piercing directness.

"Was it not there? Did I cause trouble?"

"Yes, it was there! But what made you write it down at all? Were you not aware that they are seeking my informant?" He let her go and began to pace in and out of the shadows. "If they would have caught you, they would have hanged you! Did you think of *that*?"

Stopping in front of her again, he did not give her time to answer. "Well *I* thought of it. And I haven't had a good night's sleep since!" If he had planned to speak calmly, he failed in that endeavor.

"I did not intend to make you worry," Sophia said softly.

"For not intending, you did a commendable job of it." He turned away and stared into the darkness for a moment, and then spoke over his shoulder, as if in that instant his control had been reestablished. "I'm sorry." He turned toward her more fully and paused. "I apologize. That is not why I came."

Sophia lifted her gaze and stared up at him, trying to keep her voice from quivering. "Then why?" she whispered. "It is dangerous."

"Yes, that is precisely why I am here," he said, his tone still severe. "You and your family are in great danger."

Sophia nodded and looked down so that he could not read her expression. "The Patriots this time, I suppose."

"Yes." Morgan put his hands on her shoulders again but at least the touch was gentle. His words, however, were not. "Here's what I came to tell you. You're leaving this house."

Sophia took a step back at his tone, and was seized by a wild impulse to laugh aloud. "Whatever do you mean?"

"You're going to go to Duncannon. The British can protect you there. Do you understand?"

"But you cannot just order it," she said defiantly. "Surely you do not think I have the power or the authority to make Uncle Charles pack up and leave this place."

"I have no doubt you can do it," he said, his eyes seeming to burn into hers even in the darkness. "I've come to have great confidence in your ability to get men to see your particular point of view."

Sophia took another step back and inhaled deeply before she was able to gain control again. "I do not like the insinuation."

Morgan seemed to understand that he had pushed too far, and was yet reluctant to back down on his stance. "I apologize for the insinuation," he said. "Yet still you must go."

Unable to slow her racing thoughts, Sophia turned her back to him and stared into the night sky. If the warning were real—and she had no reason to believe it was not—she and her family would be better off with the British. This house was indeed isolated and would be vulnerable to attacks by Patriots or marauders. What good would it do to waste away here far from the action of war anyway?

She sighed deeply and crossed her arms over her chest defiantly. On the other hand, she did not like being told what to do—even by someone she respected as much as Colonel Morgan. She was a civilian, after all, and not under his control.

"I prefer to form my own opinion without the aid of yours," she said defiantly. "And you are meddling in that which concerns you little."

"As to the former, that may be true, but as for the latter, you are wrong," he said, sounding serious and solemn.

Sophia turned and raised her eyes up to his, but could see he was not going to elaborate on why it concerned him. Still, she resisted the impulse to simply give into his urgings. "What if I wish to remain here? And send the rest to Duncannon for safety? I could keep my servant Mash to protect me."

"That would not change things," he said, looking deep into her eyes, "only complicate them." His tone was unusually soft and husky, and caused her heart to twitch unexpectedly in an almost painful way. He turned away abruptly, as if he feared his penetrating gaze might reveal too much.

Sophia shook her head in exasperation and began to pace as she thought about how she would carry out such a plan. "I know Uncle Charles has a business acquaintance who resides in Duncannon." She stopped beside Colonel Morgan, somewhat annoyed with herself for accepting his mandate so easily, and angry at him for making it in the first place. Yet this man seemed able to discern things by instinct in a way that no one else could analyze or understand. Perhaps she should listen to him.

"I'm sure if he understands the danger, that is where he will go."

"It needs to be tomorrow." Morgan's voice sounded low and intimidating as the moon unexpectedly sent a shaft of light to surround him, making him appear like something other than flesh and blood. "You must stress to him the urgency."

"*Tomorrow?*" Sophia frowned. "Then you know something you have not told me."

She watched a nerve throb in his cheek.

"I know you are in danger."

She threw up her hands. "However will I accomplish it?" She walked over to the bench and sat, staring into the darkness as she pondered her dilemma.

"That is for you to decide." Morgan was unyielding. "But it must be done."

Feeling helpless and rejected, Sophia suppressed the urge to break into tears only by tremendous effort of will. "Very well. I will try."

Morgan crossed his arms and looked down at her. "You must do more than *try*."

Sophia stood in one movement, angry at how he challenged and pushed her so, and yet knowing he was doing it for her own safety. "I will *do* it"—she paused and took a deep breath—"though I don't know how."

Morgan sighed as if a great weight had been lifted from his shoulders, then turned toward the fountain and stared at the shimmering reflection of the stars on the water.

Sophia wondered what it would be like to converse with this man when neither the pressure of his command or the strain of war bore down upon him.

"I'm not sure it was prudent to come all this way." Sophia stood behind him, staring at the wide breadth of his shoulders. The air was soft, and the weather pleasant with the gentle caress of a southern breeze behind them.

"Nothing between us has been prudent." He glanced over his shoulder at her with a look of impatient concern. "Why start worrying about that now?"

Sophia could never be sure if her presence provoked, perplexed, or pleased him, and tonight was no exception. One moment he seemed caring, and the next, angry or sullen. What was it that drove him at times to be so indifferent and detached? He seemed to prefer remaining a stranger, being unapproachable and beyond her reach.

She wondered if it was to protect her. Or torture her?

Sophia shook her head in exasperation. Although his presence seemed somehow familiar and comfortable, there was something about being with him that felt both exciting and dangerous. She walked up beside him and watched the water splashing from the fountain. "I'm sorry I made you angry."

"Not angry," he said without hesitation. "Just concerned."

"I could think of no other way to pass on the information."

Morgan turned toward her and reached for her hand. "Please, Miss Adair. No matter the circumstances, don't ever write anything down again." It was not a request. There was steel in the soft, rasping voice. Yet in the pressure of his hand, Sophia felt both a strength and gentleness, as if she were absorbing the soft, welcoming warmth of embers rather than those from a flaming fire.

Sophia took a deep breath, trying to steady herself against the feelings that consumed her. The garden was a solemn, quiet place, yet suddenly seemed alive with meanings, hints, and whispers.

Standing there beneath the velvety sky full of stars, thoughts of war seemed to melt away as utter peacefulness enveloped her. For once she heard no crackling spit of skirmishing parties, no thumping of distant war drums, or echoes of galloping horses bringing dispatches from afar. Everything felt serene—the intense quietness making it feel more like a dream than reality.

It appeared Colonel Morgan sensed it too, and did not seem willing to interrupt the perfect sensation of being completely isolated from the world and its troubles. For moments that stretched into minutes he did not venture to break the silence or disturb the sanctity of the surroundings with speech.

Gazing into his eyes, Sophia felt a strange connection— almost an attraction— to him. How else to explain this warm, sweet weight on her heart that throbbed like raw, pulsing pain? He appeared a tower of strength to her, solid, competent, and commanding, but something in his face told of gentleness and of passionate. The look made her regret even more that she had caused him to worry, and had added to the heavy responsibility of his duties.

For just a moment Sophia allowed herself to ponder what it would be like if the two of them were not weighted down by their duties. What would Colonel Morgan be like if he could detach himself from the obligations of war and stand here unrestrained?

When she returned her attention to him, she felt the color begin to rise in her cheeks. The way his eyes rested on her, she had the distinct feeling he had just read her mind.

Colonel Morgan took a long, deep breath and let it out after a long pause. "I suppose I shall have to use discretion here." His eyes were darkly tender as he studied her face with an absorbed, thoughtful look. His expression was soothing in its power of restraint, but it seemed to take great effort for him to keep his look and his tone emotionless now.

Sophia did not know if he was talking to her or trying to convince himself of the need for discretion. She felt unable to move as he placed his hand on her cheek, staring at her with a gaze so intent that it seemed to draw her toward him with an irresistible force.

The look lasted only an instant. In the span of a heartbeat, he withdrew and turned away, terminating the moment and the conversation. His deportment changed too, from gentle and compassionate to composed and resolute. "I need to get back. I'll trust you with your word, Miss Adair."

There was no time to say more, nor did Sophia answer with words. But as Colonel Morgan turned to leave, his eyes spoke a language eloquent enough for once to assure her of what he was thinking.

# CHAPTER 9

*I shall not die without a hope that light and liberty are on a steady advance.*

- THOMAS JEFFERSON

*A*s Colonel Morgan rode up the lane to the plantation house he'd been using as headquarters, he discovered the Continentals had arrived during his brief absence. Tents were sprawled hither and yon across the fields and into the forest bordering the edges of the swampland. An impatient-looking officer stood on the porch of the house watching as he rode in.

"Colonel Morgan, I presume?"

"Yes, I am Colonel Morgan." Morgan accepted the man's extended hand. "I heard you were coming, General Wells. We're much obliged for the extra help."

"From what I've been told, you've been doing a pretty good job on your own." The corpulent officer moved with

Morgan to the doorway. "I understand the British have taken off to Duncannon."

Morgan nodded. "They have no choice. We've made it impossible for them to get supplies here."

"That's what I understand." The general stepped into the foyer and started to unbutton his coat. "They took the worst of the Tories with them too. Couldn't ask for a better situation."

"Sir?" Morgan began to get an uncomfortable feeling, which Wells must have noticed.

"Colonel, if you don't mind me saying so, it looks like you've spent half the last month in your clothes and most of those in the saddle." The general patted him on the shoulder. "Why don't you go get some rest, and we'll discuss my strategy in the morning."

Morgan looked down at his dirty and disheveled attire. "Is it that obvious?"

General Wells laughed. "You're going to like my plan, Colonel. It's bold and audacious—and you're just the man to help pull it off. Go get some rest so you're ready."

Morgan did not argue. He couldn't. His whole weary body hailed the approach of some much-needed repose.

Colonel Morgan came back to consciousness early the next morning, as wide awake as any man could be after five hours of dog-tired sleep. General Wells and his staff appeared not long after, and the council of war soon commenced.

General Wells stood over the table set in the middle of the room, looking down at the map that had been placed there. "Are you familiar with Duncannon, Colonel Morgan?"

"Yes, I know it's general location."

"I mean the terrain around the town. Are you familiar enough to position artillery?"

Morgan had just taken a sip of tea, and it was only with great effort that he kept from choking on it.

I am, sir," one of Morgan's men answered before he had a chance to catch his breath. "I'm from that section."

"Why do you ask?" Morgan attempted to steady his hand as he put down his tea, but it still clanked noisily when it came in contact with the desk.

"Isn't it obvious? We've got the Redcoats and all the damn Tories in the town. We're going to hit them with everything we have."

Morgan swallowed hard, as if trying to dislodge something stuck in his throat. "But there are families in that town. *Women.*"

No one, of course, understood what caused his voice to vibrate so deeply. All anyone saw was a look of pain mixed with grim determination on the face of a man who had already worked so hard and given so much.

"*Tory* women!" Wells exclaimed. "Worse than their husbands and twice the trouble."

"You can say that again," Captain Tate said under his breath as he leaned against the wall.

"No need to worry." Wells walked over and put his hand on Morgan's shoulder. "You and your men have done such an outstanding job in setting this trap that I'm giving you the easy assignment of shelling it from the perimeter. You won't even had to get your hands dirty—just obliterate them from afar. My troops will do the dangerous work of rounding up the devils."

A sudden revulsion of feeling made Morgan dizzy and weak, and threatened to overwhelm him. He'd told Sophia Adair to go to Duncannon, had *ordered* her to do so with all haste. Certainly by now she had fled to the safe harbor of that town, defenseless and unaware of the danger that was imminent.

He took a deep breath and let it out slowly, as he rallied his strength. The general's order was one that could not be questioned, and in defense of his country, he was not the type of man to refuse to respond. He nodded his head, and despite the nausea that rose in his throat, he agreed to the plan of attack.

Morgan watched as some of his men sat sleepily on their horses observing the chaos of the ranks falling into line as the last blue wisps of smoke from their dying campfires filled the air.

The warmth of the rising sun wrapped around his shoulders and the sound of twittering birds resounded, but Morgan didn't notice. He was remembering their last meeting—the language, the touch, the tone. The entire scene, with all its peaceful surroundings, remained indelibly impressed upon his memory, so that even now, try as he might to stop it, her voice still resounded in his ears.

Only three days had passed since then, and now Morgan had been tasked with placing his two pieces of artillery alongside others brought by General Wells. If he could have found a possible pretext for refusing obedience he would gladly have done so, but that was not how he was made. War was not logical, nor was it just, and being a soldier wasn't always easy, nor was it fair.

As the men continued to gather, nothing could be heard but the creaking of the saddles, and the horses stirring restlessly. The men waited while Morgan stood gazing straight ahead, steady, composed, as he tried to master himself and the situation. He did not feel despair any more, only regret—deep enough to be regarded as pain.

When General Wells ordered him to fire, Morgan obeyed, launching his power upon the town in his customary fashion. It appeared as if the buildings were being hit with a mighty gale of iron hail that no one and nothing could survive. The reverberation of sound came back to the hill where he stood, mingling into one great roar, like the sweep of a tornado over a forest of giant trees.

The shells continued to fly, but Morgan did not hear them. There was shouting and yelling when the tops of buildings began to catch fire or disappear altogether, but he did not hear that either.

He stood with one foot on a rock, with no coat and no regard to temperature or danger, staring silently at the town with a remote expression upon his face. Remaining in this recklessly exposed position, he was the one officer who never cheered, but closely followed each shot as it buried itself in some building. No one knew why he stood watching each missile so anxiously, or why he only pressed his lips more tightly as if enduring a private torture when it exploded near a house.

The roar, the hiss, and the crash of shells continued to blend in one dreadful chorus with a horror hard to express. Sometimes the explosion would throw fragments of what it destroyed in the air: dirt, boards, bricks, and rocks. Through stifling smoke Morgan watched it all, a grand yet sorrowful scene that threatened to tear his heart from his soul.

As they defended the town and its inhabitants, the British and the Tories made a strong defense of their own, firing back at the enemy. But the defensive stance only cost them more men, as Morgan brought his guns to bear on the parts of town he now knew were inhabited by enemy forces.

"Sir you are unnecessarily exposed here," one of the men told him. "Won't you step back?"

Morgan never turned around to address the man, but spoke as if in a trance, his eyes lit with an unearthly glow of conviction. "If you are afraid, you are at liberty to step back."

At night, the sky appeared red from the great conflagration of the town, and at dawn, Morgan stood again at his post, searching the horizon, his eyes suffused with private anguish.

Never did a man gaze on a more dismal, ghastly scene than was revealed by those first gray gleams showing in the east. Wherever one looked, the vista was the same, an endless stretch of utter desolation and devastation. The town appeared inhabitable and unpeopled. As for visible motion, there was none—not one bird, beast, or living creature in sight.

Morgan stared at the destruction in silence, though his heart throbbed with restless urgency as the sun drew higher in the sky. If he could just know she was safe.

This torturous uncertainty would surely kill him.

Sophia knelt upon the bench near the railing, and looked out at the moon half hidden by a fast-moving bank of clouds. Except for a faraway whinny of a horse, the night was quiet, with a hush so heavy that she felt nothing could disturb her peaceful thoughts.

Her mind drifted to the last time she had seen Colonel Morgan, and then to the engagement and resulting destruction of Duncannon. Had he worried she might be there? Or had he gone on with his business accepting her as a necessary casualty of war?

Her heart skipped a beat as she thought of the one other possibility she had heretofore blocked from her mind. Had he sent her there intentionally, knowing the Americans would be attacking and turning the town to rubble? He had seemed so adamant about her immediate departure. She shuddered at the prospect he might have welcomed the opportunity to be completely relieved of her.

If that was the case, then she was glad she had discovered that her uncle had already been making preparations to abandon the Spangler home and move his family to Duncannon with no encouragement from her. At the last moment however, he had changed his plans and moved into an unoccupied plantation near the town instead.

Surprisingly enough, Colonel Tyndale and his troops, including Major Briggs, had vacated Duncannon ahead of the bombardment as well, as if they had been forewarned. She was once again surrounded by a sea of Redcoats encamped on the grounds and fields of Kensington Hall, where she now resided.

With all of the upheaval, Sophia had considered giving up the facade and heading to the nearest Patriot camp. But now that the British were this close again, duty made her stay. She could do little from an American camp. Here is where she could inflict the most damage.

"Daydreaming again, Sophia?" Sophia jumped and looked behind her. She had not even heard the footsteps of Major Briggs behind her.

She forced a laugh and turned back toward the velvety darkness. She did not wish to speak to this man whose eyes took such liberties. "Just enjoying the night sky. It's—"

"All you do these days is daydream," Briggs said. "May I indulge myself and believe it is with thoughts of me?"

Startled, Sophia turned her head, raised her eyes to his darkening gaze, then stood and moved away from him. She had started to fear the looks he gave her, and his attentions were so bold of late that she no longer tried to hide her dislike of him. She knew that her aunt and uncle thought him a suitable match, but she did not wish to give him any incentive or offer the impression she agreed with the arrangement.

Briggs must have read her expression of disgust and loathing. "Perhaps you like a certain American officer better?" His tone was cold and threatening.

Sophia tried to catch her breath as she whirled around to face him. "What are you talking about?"

"The American officer. Colonel Morgan. Perhaps *he* is the one you're dreaming about."

"Major Briggs, I do believe you're trying to insult me." Sophia could feel the heat rising in her cheeks, and hoped he would assume it was from anger.

"Yes, that would be an insult, wouldn't it? You, a girl of standing, thinking about a low-down, dirty rebel. It is almost too difficult to fathom."

Sophia tried to act undisturbed, but his slur against the Americans was too much. "A man with an evil smell takes offence at every wrinkled nose," she said. "Perhaps you have cause to be sensitive." She started to walk away, back into the house, but he grabbed her arm and whirled her around.

"Mary told me, so there's no use denying it."

Sophia laughed. "Mary told you what? That I like to daydream?"

"She told me that ever since you returned from the American camp you've been in a trance."

"Mary talks too much." Sophia stared at him with slanted, angry eyes. "We both know she exaggerates everything."

"She knows you better than anyone," he sneered. "Look how you tremble."

"I'm trembling because you're hurting me. And scaring me. Let me go!"

Briggs only brought her closer and whispered in her ear. "I am not without sentiment."

"Yes, it's principles you lack," Sophia said, as she struggled free from his grasp and ran to the door. Pausing with her hand on the latch, she tried to catch her breath and compose herself. "I'm very disappointed in you, Major Briggs," she said, hoping to end any future advances by him. "That was highly inappropriate."

He merely smiled. "Highly inappropriate perhaps to you, but quite enjoyable to me."

Sophia turned and shot him look of disgust. "I believe you have lost what little honor, if any, that you once possessed."

"I've lost nothing," she heard him say in a low, sinister voice as she proceeded into the house. The rest of his words were muffled when she slammed the door behind her, yet she heard them nonetheless. "Mark my words, one of these days you will treat me with the regard that I deserve."

# CHAPTER 10

*Doing what good we can; when we cannot do all we would wish.*
- THOMAS JEFFERSON, 1803

*D*ays and weeks had slipped by almost unnoticed as autumn began to drop her vivid drapery, withdrawing slowly but perceptibly. Sophia wrapped her cloak more tightly around her as dried leaves darted and danced across the path in front of her. The sight of them scurrying hither and fro like playful children did not lighten her mood. The distance she had traveled by foot was only a few miles, but the time that had passed felt like an eternity.

Sophia glanced up at the nearly absent moon but did not stop walking. Covered by clouds, it cast very little light, possessing no power to dissolve the dark foreboding that continued to stalk her.

Thinking back to the violent sunset she had witnessed earlier, she tried to discount the vision and suppress her belief in omens. The deep crimson sky had been both beautiful and eerie, and the windblown trees to the west had appeared to writhe and dance against the backdrop of the bloody-looking sky. Whether it was the boughs nodding and whispering mysteriously to one another as she passed or the cool night air that made her shiver, she did not care to dwell upon.

When the slim moon finally broke through the bank of clouds for a moment, Sophia stopped to get her bearings. Squinting into the darkness as the wind whipped and pulled at her skirt, she heard the sound of rustling leaves, broken occasionally by the lonely wail of two tree limbs rubbing together.

She started to walk again, using the light from above to add a new swiftness to her stride. At last, just ahead, she made out the jagged outline of the building she sought. Then, like a candle being extinguished, all became dark again.

Sophia's heart increased its rapid pace at the thought that Colonel Morgan may have arrived at the rendezvous place before her. Not being familiar with the area, she had wandered off the trail, and lost all track of time. Taking a deep breath, she continued toward the house, keeping to the shadows and moving without a sound. She could not shake the feeling that some great evil, some impending awful event was about to occur.

Up the sagging porch steps she trod, pausing at each loud groan, her heart beating tumultuously in her ears. As she turned the large brass doorknob and gave a hesitant push, the door groaned loudly, like a distressed warning about something ominous within.

Again she paused, straining for the slightest sound that would validate the sense of foreboding that overwhelmed her. Hearing nothing, she took a step inside and felt the stagnant, stale air press down upon her. Sophia stood silently within, trying to calm her rapid heartbeat, and quell the suffocating sensation that made it difficult to breathe.

Not until she closed the door behind her did she become aware that she was not alone. A shadow emerged from a corner and began forming into the shape of a man right before her eyes. Without warning, the low glow of a single tallow candle illuminated the room, and the blunt shape detached itself from the darkness and stood before her.

"Sophia, you disappoint me." Major Briggs strode over to a small desk and sat upon it while gazing at her with slant-eyed viciousness. His eyes sparkled unnaturally, perhaps with liquor, for the smell of alcohol now permeated the room.

Sophia could not have been more astonished had a dark spirit risen from the ashes of the empty fireplace and turned its ruthless gaze in her direction. She did not answer nor did she move. She stood frozen in desperate and helpless panic as she tried to calm her thrashing heart.

She heard, rather than saw, Briggs take a step toward her and felt, rather than observed, his threatening attitude. When Sophia lifted her eyes to meet his, he laughed at her, as if taking great delight in seeing her expression of fearful, speechless surprise, and watching her throat as she tried to swallow.

She wished desperately to hide and scramble for cover in a room where none existed. She stood trembling, held in place by the mere presence of his dark stare.

"You cannot imagine with what anticipation I have been waiting for this moment," Briggs said, his eyes emitting the eager, merciless gleam of a bird of prey about to grasp its quarry.

Sophia had always disliked—but never really feared—this man. Yet now she stood paralyzed and insensible with fright. "It was *you* who summoned me here?"

"Yes, such I grieve to say for your sake is the case." He sat on the desk with his arms crossed as he studied her, speaking with a sort of ominous satisfaction. "You were, of course, expecting someone else."

Sophia remained silent, but she felt a cold hand clutch her vitals as he gazed at her. His eyes seemed to shine a bright light on her, exposing her secrets and her thoughts. Earlier she had been practically panting, but now she struggled just to draw breath.

He cleared his throat. "Yes, a pity I could not do this at Kensington Hall, but the circumstances such as they are—"

"What is it you want?" Sophia knew she was alone and far away from anyone who could help her, but now that the element of surprise had worn off, her survival instincts began to take over. Grim necessity forced her to be strong. Composure began to settle upon her

"Is it not obvious, Miss Adair?" Briggs pushed himself off the desk and walked toward her. When he stood directly in front of her, he leaned down and whispered in her ear. "I want *you*."

Sophia took a step back, shaking her head in confusion. "I do not understand."

"Allow me to explain my dear." He spoke in a low, threatening tone. "Our positions are now somewhat reversed. It is poetic justice that you are threatened with a taste of the downfall you schemed for me and the British army."

Sophia cast her eyes to the floor, lest he read the fear in them. It was impossible to take his words for anything other than their full intent. He had discovered she was a spy, and he was waiting for her to admit it. "You are not making sense, Major Briggs." It was all she could think of to say. "I do not understand what you want."

"It's very simple really." He sounded almost jovial. "I want you to go back to Kensington Hall and tell everyone that you have at last come to your senses—that you have agreed to wed me." He took a step closer, but she kept her attention on the floor. "And then I am going to come and collect you as my bride." He paused for a moment as he watched her raise her defiant gaze. "Using force if necessary."

"Then with *force* shall you be met."

Sophia took a hurried step back when his face turned red with rage.

"You arrogant little rebel-loving chit! Preferring an American officer to *me*! Tonight I will have complete capitulation, my little traitor."

"I do not know what you are talking about," Sophia said, trying to keep her voice from shaking.

"Come now, Sophia. Surely you were aware of the misery evoked when you raised your treasonous hand against the British government." He stood before her, breathing hard, his eyes burning with fury.

Sophia studied him for a moment, trying to figure out if he was bluffing or had discovered her secret. In the space of heartbeat, it became obvious that he knew, forcing her to y necessity, her mind grew calmer, though it was a calmness borne of hopelessness.

"If you refer to treason as attempting to shake off the yoke of a tyrannical government, then it is an acceptable term to use," she said, looking him in the eye. "I deem it a flattery to be classed with those who are willing to sacrifice all against such oppression."

Briggs sucked in his breath as if she had physically punched him. "You make a mockery of our monarch!"

"Surely you do not believe I would follow the edicts declared by the wicked soul of a worthless king." Sophia spoke forcefully. "I fight not to enslave but to set a country free." She crossed her arms and turned her back on him. "Take what revenge you please. I have done what I was compelled to do as a patriot, and I'm ready for the consequences, be what they may."

She heard Briggs take a deep breath, and when he spoke, he sounded calm and gentle. "You must know how much I care for you, Sophia."

Sophia stiffened with frigid repulse at his tone, for it sounded more dangerous and vile than his anger and rage. She guessed what he was going to say next, yet the words, when they came, horrified her.

"You are a woman and a spy," he whispered, standing slightly behind her. "I profoundly esteem the one and will freely forgive the other—as your husband."

When she whirled around to face him in protest, he placed his finger to her lips. "Hush, my darling. I have caught you red-handed thinking you were meeting an American officer. Without my protection as your husband, you will hang."

"Then I will hang." Sophia had no hesitation in her voice, making it clear a rope was more appealing to her than a life with him.

Briggs's eyes flashed with anger, but now that he possessed the upper hand, he instantly calmed himself. "Not so fast. I have not yet revealed my conditions."

"No matter your conditions—"

Sophia was unable to finish her sentence. He grabbed a handful of her hair, and tilted her head back so she was forced to look into his evil eyes.

"You have nowhere to turn and no one to turn to," he snarled. "You are powerless and will obey me."

"I will obey my conscience." She kept her unwavering eyes locked on his, and for a moment, feared he was going to strike her.

But once again he summoned his composure and merely laughed as he released his grip. "Miss Adair, you do not seem to understand two small points."

Sophia raised her head a notch and eyed him warily. "Which are?"

He leaned down to within inches of her face. "You live at my pleasure. You die when I chose."

Despite her rapidly beating heart, Sophia held her ground. "As I said before, Major Briggs, I am willing"—she paused a moment—"to die, I mean."

Briggs stared at her with slant-eyed disbelief, but then calmly reached out and fingered a strand of her hair as if contemplating some evil deed. "In a few moments, other factors will be revealed that, I believe, will make you change your mind." He brought his finger up to caress her face, and she turned her head to avoid it.

"There is nothing in this world that will make me change my mind."

"Oh, yes, my darling, there will be a wedding tonight." He dropped his hand from her face to finger a gun holstered at his side. "Or a funeral tomorrow."

"Then let me be clear as well, Major Briggs." Sophia did not try to hide her anger or revulsion. "If there is a wedding, it will be over my dead body."

"Do not be so hasty, Miss Adair." He paused and walked around her, as if sizing up a prized horse. "I believe I know you better than that, and did not say the funeral would be for you. You will accept my hand in marriage, if you value *his* life."

Sophia's heart plummeted to her feet as she jerked her head back to meet his gaze. "What do you mean? Is he here?" Her throat was suddenly so dry she could barely form the words.

"Ah, so you know to whom I refer." There was a gleam of terrible menace in his eye as he walked in front of the candle, casting a huge and grotesque shadow on the wall. "In anticipation of your stubbornness, I decided upon a punishment that would be as pleasurable for me to inflict as it would be painful for you to endure."

He paused a moment, as if waiting for his words to sink in. "If my calculations are correct, he will be here shortly."

Sophia blinked hard to fight the tears she felt welling within her. She had seen the potential consequences of her espionage coming, had felt it, perhaps even expected it—but she never thought it would involve Colonel Morgan.

Before she had time to respond, Briggs placed his large hand across her mouth. "Quiet! I hear someone coming."

Sophia strained her ears, but heard only the ominous moaning of the wind. Then, from out of the darkness came the distinct sound of a horse. As she stood listening to the steady approach, she felt the shock of each hoof beat stabbing her heart.

With evil precision, Briggs pressed a gun to her throat and whispered, "Do not say a word, or he is a dead man. This house is surrounded. If you play along with my little game, he will not be harmed."

"You will release him?" Sophia could barely form the words.

"It is you I want," he whispered, as he moved out of the light. "Quiet now."

Sophia stood rigid, listening to the footsteps approach, all the while feeling as if poisonous vapors had risen in the room to wreath and curl around her. Yesterday she would have said it was her desire to see Colonel Morgan again more than anything in the world—and now it was the last thing she wanted.

She felt the blood drain from her face as she envisioned the fate that awaited her. Yet she had a strangely detached feeling, as if standing a long way off and watching someone else in the slow throes of death. Her courage and resolve, confronted by that which she could neither overcome nor endure, had receded in hasty flight, leaving only numbness in its wake

As the footsteps on the porch grew nearer, the wind outside seemed to sob. Within moments the door opened, groaning loudly again as if from a personal pain.

# CHAPTER 11

*Therefore put on the full armor of God, so that when the day of evil comes, you may be able to stand your ground, and after you have done everything, to stand.*
- Ephesians 6:12-13

Colonel Morgan appeared in the doorway looking mud-splattered and careworn as he regarded Sophia cautiously without moving. For a few long moments he resembled a statue standing there without life or breath. Yet even in the dim light, she discerned a deadly intent in his eyes.

"I came as soon as I received your message." His face revealed a mixture of agitation and concern as he stepped in her direction.

Sophia stared at him in grievous confusion as she put the pieces of the puzzle together. Major Briggs had penned a communication to her and to Colonel Morgan, making it appear they had summoned each other to this rendezvous. It had never occurred to her the writing was not Morgan's. Scrawled and barely legible, she had only supposed it had been written at night or in a great hurry—which had only served to give urgency to her travels.

Before she could speak, or even meet Morgan's gaze, Briggs stepped out of the shadows and into the ghastly light.

"Welcome, Colonel Morgan. Thanks to our mutual friend, Miss Adair, we finally meet face-to-face."

Colonel Morgan blinked once in surprise before his expression turned to one of angry disappointment. He glanced at Briggs without acknowledging his presence and then shifted his attention to Sophia, his eyes gravely questioning.

Sophia knew it was useless to dispute the claim—even if she had the breath within her to try—so she stood dazed, unmoving, as if waiting to be released from a sorcerer's spell.

From the look on his face, it appeared Colonel Morgan had never completely trusted her—perhaps assumed she had been working with the British all along. The fact that the Spanglers had retired to the safety of Kensington Hall instead of Duncannon, as he had ordered, surely suggested —and perhaps substantiated—his suspicions about her.

Sophia acknowledged his reaction with a defiant lift of her chin. What did it matter? He had never declared any interest in her. Perhaps she should take some consolation in the fact that his lack of compassion would make this whole horrible lie much easier.

From the corner of her eye, Sophia noticed the faint glow of the moon as it burst from beneath its cover, throwing ghastly shadows on the floor around her. The light seemed to linger in Morgan's eyes as he looked around the room, perhaps trying to understand how he came to be a pawn in a game he knew nothing about.

"I don't believe we've met." Colonel Morgan turned his attention to Briggs. "I have the honor of addressing …."

"I am Major Malcolm Briggs in the service of His Majesty's forces." The British officer did not attempt to conceal his aversion. "I fought you once—at Brewster."

"Really? I don't remember much fighting from your side," Morgan replied, with the slightest air of mockery to his tone. He made a slight attempt at a bow. "A pleasure, I'm sure, Major Briggs. Although I've not had the honor of your acquaintance, I am no stranger to your character and reputation."

Again, the words were said pleasantly enough, yet in such a way as to imply that Briggs's character and reputation were not things of which to be proud.

With a low roar commencing in her ears, Sophia glanced up at Morgan. He stood with a look of subdued humor in his eyes, perfectly calm and unruffled at finding himself in these unforeseen circumstances.

"If we're going to examine each other's character, let's start with yours," Briggs remarked savagely. "I do not like to be treated with disrespect even by those for whom I have little regard.

Sophia sucked in some air, but could think of nothing to say that would not jeopardize Morgan or incriminate herself. She slid her gaze to the window, trying to remove herself from the room by watching patchy shafts of moonlight play on the ground.

"Are you all right, Miss Adair?" Sophia heard the words as if they were coming to her through the mists of time. She glanced up at Colonel Morgan who regarded her with reckless, challenging eyes. "You look rather pale."

For the first time, Sophia was seized with a sense of despair that bordered on mortal dread. Her eyes glanced from the vindictive face of Major Briggs, whom she loathed, to the grave, composed face of Colonel Morgan, whom she greatly esteemed, and then turned to the candle and focused on the flickering flame.

She could not speak for fear her voice would tremble or her eyes would reveal her lies. For his safety, she must succeed in hiding her true feelings no matter how much she wished otherwise. This secret yearning of her heart must remain unuttered. For his sake, and his sake alone, her lips were vowed to silence.

"I find it interesting that you have so much interest in my *betrothed.*" Briggs's voice cut through her like a sharp knife. "If I were the jealous type I would officially tender a challenge."

Morgan's eyes shot back to Sophia, and he stared at her for some seconds that seemed more like hours. "Does he speak the truth?" His tone turned low and grave. He looked and acted as if he had been struck with a bullet.

Briggs walked behind her and put his hand on her shoulder as if to remind her of his threat. Seeing no escape from the impending doom, Sophia nerved herself to the ordeal, but it took everything within her not to cringe or step away.

"Oh, I believe I've gone and spoiled the surprise." Briggs squeezed her shoulder with a firm grasp. "Tell him, darling."

Sophia could not bear to look into Colonel Morgan's eyes and so she stared at the flame and nodded. After a silence that seemed to last an eternity, she murmured. "It is true."

After saying the words, Sophia felt a finality that she was not ready to admit—or willing to accept. When she found the courage to look at Colonel Morgan again, he appeared speechless, seeming to doubt the evidence of his own eyes. Yet a strange gravity had settled upon his face, unlike any look she had ever seen.

Turning her attention back to the candle flame, Sophia

stood in an agony of contending emotions. He was staring at her, she could tell. She felt her chin tremble, but she did not allow her eyes to waver or show any sign of the grief that consumed her. Wild thoughts ran through her head and a scream trembled on her lips, but he must never know what she did to set him free.

At last Colonel Morgan spoke. "I apologize for the intrusion," he said with cold and unemotional authority, "but there is some confusion. Was I not summoned here?" His tone was harsh, utterly unlike what she was accustomed to hearing.

Briggs stepped forward. "It is a wish that I granted my bride." He turned his head to take in Sophia's expression, and then turned back to Morgan. "I do not question her motives, but I believe she wished to tell you the news herself. I apologize for ruining her announcement."

"I see." Morgan eyed her noncommittally, but a flicker of pain crossed his face before he mastered it. "Then allow me to be the first to congratulate you."

In the span of a heartbeat he had effortlessly regained control again, sounding so calm and unmoved that his words produced a twinge of pain in her, like that of a twisting knife. Sophia had been willing to make this sacrifice because she esteemed this man, but it hit her like a violent wave that she also loved him. It had happened slowly, and yet inevitably, this yielding of her spirit to his. And now, to observe the aversion in his eyes as he gazed upon her was almost more than she could bear.

Sophia stood silently, staring at the dimly lit cobwebs hanging over the mantel, wondering if God would help her keep this horrible secret or if the pain in her heart would force her to divulge it all—though it would mean death to them both.

The feelings that had blossomed for Colonel Morgan

during their dangerous interludes brought more agony than the thought of death, because this lie and his acceptance of it could never be reconciled. The man who stared at her with such cold indifference, the voice that carried disdain in its tone of congratulation would reverberate in her heart and mind as long as she lived.

It now became so silent that one would have fancied the room was empty. Although she could feel tears rebelling insolently against her will, Sophia dared not shed them—not with his life at stake. In a few minutes it would all be over. She must keep her thoughts and desires concealed from him for just a little while longer. Easing her gaze over to him, she tried to memorize every line and feature of his strong face, even as he stared at her with cold, ice-blue eyes.

The sound of a horse and carriage arriving in front of the building interrupted her thoughts.

Briggs pulled out a timepiece, consulted it, and clapped his hands together. "My, how time has flown. Being a considerate and thoughtful groom, I've arranged a ride back to Kensington Hall for you." He grinned maliciously. "I'll walk you out." He turned toward Morgan and nodded, terminating any further conversation. "Excuse us, please."

Sophia felt dazed and somewhat unsteady as she pictured the final grains of sand trickling through the hourglass of her life. She was just about to turn and follow Briggs when Morgan stepped forward and took her hand, grasping it with more pressure than was either wise or polite.

"Did you think I'd rest content without a farewell?" His expression may have been carved from stone and his eyes were as inscrutable as ever, yet Sophia felt he was trying to tell her something.

Without warning Sophia noticed two British soldiers enter the room from a door behind Morgan, looking threatening and full of menace. When she opened her mouth to alert him, Briggs took her by the arm. "Shall we go?" It was posed politely as a question, but the firm hand told her otherwise. She tried to look over Morgan's shoulder to see what was happening, but someone from within slammed the door behind her, blocking her view.

# CHAPTER 12

*Nothing is so strong as gentleness: nothing so gentle as real strength.*
- St. Francis de Sales

The man driving the carriage appeared to take no notice of Sophia, but nodded at Briggs as he helped her into her seat. "Have a safe journey, my love. I'll see you soon." Major Briggs smiled mockingly as he began to close the door, but Sophia stopped him. "You will not harm him," she said as unemotionally as she could. "You gave your word you would release him."

"Of course, my dear." The grin he shot her made her cringe. "He will be released once we are wed. Now hurry on to Kensington and prepare for me. I'll be along shortly."

He started to close the door, but she grabbed his hand. "You realize I am asking a polite favor," she said, forcing a smile, "not making a demand."

Briggs seemed surprised at her sudden kindness and

patted her hand as if she were a child. "No need to worry, darling."

As soon as the door clicked shut, the driver rapped the reins on the horses' backs and they were off. Sophia sat back in the seat and closed her eyes, but could not relax. Never had twenty-four hours stretched out before her in a span that seemed so immeasurable and unending.

She would be married within a day to a man she despised. Her life would never be the same. And yet she could take some consolation in the fact that no matter what became of her, she had spared the life of Colonel Grant Morgan.

Sophia breathed slowly and not very deeply against the pressing ache in her chest. When her hand grew numb to the fingertips, she realized she was gripping the side of the carriage as it lurched over the rutty road. She heard the faint sound of a dog barking nearby, but it soon faded away, leaving nothing but the clatter of the horses as they trotted methodically down the rough and uneven road.

It seemed they had only just begun their journey when the carriage slowed and then came to a complete stop. Knowing they could not possibly be at their destination, Sophia opened the door and saw the faint outline of people milling about. A murmuring of many voices, sounding to her like a beehive of activity, arose from the darkness. Along a row of trees stood the dark shadows of dozens of men and horses.

"Why have we stopped?" she demanded of the driver.

"I'm resting the horses," he answered gruffly.

Sophia's heart dropped. "But we are not yet at Kensington Hall!" She sounded anxious and shrill even to her own ears. "We must keep going!"

Her only thought was what the delay might mean for

Colonel Morgan. She had to arrive at Kensington Hall for the wedding or all would be lost. Briggs would think she had double-crossed him.

"But the horses are still fresh," she argued with the man. She thought of what Briggs would do if she did not arrive at Kensington Hall on time. He would never have the patience to learn the full account.

"I'm just following orders, miss." The man seemed completely indifferent to her concern as he casually tied off the reins.

"Whose orders?" she screamed as pure terror and panic seized her.

"*My* orders, Miss Adair."

Sophia whirled around and watched Colonel Morgan striding toward her with the calm, confident look of a steadfast soldier. Walking tall and erect with martial bearing, he had a monstrous-looking long rifle in each hand, a hatchet dangling from a belt on his waist, and a grim smile upon his face. She had never laid eyes upon a more physically imposing man.

"My apologies for the lack of ceremony," he said, stopping in front of her. "I've not had a lot of practice rescuing damsels in distress." He paused and studied her a moment. "Remember?"

He seemed to be trying to make a joke about a conversation they'd had upon their first meeting, but Sophia stood trying to decide if she were asleep or awake, dead or alive. She looked back over her shoulder from where they had come, toward where she had last seen him, and then back again, thinking he would surely disappear in that space of time. Yet he still stood there, staring at her now with a look of impatient concern. "But how—"

"I took a shortcut," he said matter-of-factly now. "I'll explain later."

The commanding attitude assumed by Morgan and the authoritative tone of his voice, did not fail in their effect on Sophia. She removed her gaze from him and began to take in her surroundings. A few candles cast a dim light from what appeared to be a small, stone church, but outside all was dark. Moonlight revealed only the dusky moving forms of men hard at work, their stern faces and rifle barrels gleaming eerily in the subdued light. From the corner of her eye she saw the driver of the carriage taking off the red coat he wore and dashing it to the ground as if it were repugnant to him.

"We're going to make a stand here if they come." Colonel Morgan's voice fell again upon her ears, sounding as reassuring and calm as if he were telling her the menu for dinner. She stared incredulously as she beheld the potent aura of the man—a vibrant power that captivated her as much as overwhelmed her. It seemed that whether in repose or in action, his eyes were lit with fire, his bearing always personifying a man carried away by duty.

"*If* they come?" Sophia felt like she was in a trance, unable to speak or think, but merely repeat his words. How could he stand there so solitary and strong in the midst of all this chaos?

"*When* they come," he said, correcting himself while gazing at her with a look of calm authority. He raised his eyes to stare musingly at the road behind her. "I fear we will not long be idle here."

"But… you can't. I mean, they're after *me*." Sophia knew Morgan did not have enough men to defend against what the British could bring to fight him. A shiver ran down her spine as she realized he probably had very little time to regroup and certainly no place to hide. To advance was unthinkable, to attempt to retrace their steps without encountering their foe, impossible. Disaster was approaching, inevitably and soon.

Her gaze drifted back to the church, to the men hard at work fortifying their positions. They toiled steadily, and by no means leisurely, in preparation for what was to come. When she returned her attention to Morgan and studied his face, it seemed to say what words could not. There would be no quarter for either of them—or any of them. They wouldn't be fighting to hold ground, but to survive. Safety lay in victory alone.

"They'll have to walk over my dead body to touch you." He no longer sounded jovial, yet neither did he sound troubled. He seemed calm and collected, as if facing death was nothing out of the ordinary for him.

She knew he had every reason to be exhausted, yet he did not appear conscious of the slightest need for rest. She recognized within him a steadiness, a shielding comfort, and the imposing force of command.

Something inside Sophia thumped violently, nearly choking her, as if a lighted match that had lain dormant in her heart had at last sparked something in her soul. It flickered and flared, leaving in its wake a reassuring feeling of peaceful certainty.

"Can you shoot one of these?" Morgan said in his next breath, holding up one of the guns. "Or load one? I'll teach you."

Such a question, following after such things as she had endured, was too much for Sophia's nerves. Morgan took another step toward her, but his figure began to dissolve before her eyes, appearing like a vapor with no beginning and no end.

"Sophia, look at me," he ordered, his voice no longer calm. She saw him drop the guns and reach for her, and was surprised and comforted by both his strength and speed. "Don't—"

That was the last thing Sophia remembered before a huge wave of disbelief—and relief—washed over her and swept her away.

# CHAPTER 13

*The consciousness of having discharged that duty which we owe to our country is superior to all other considerations.*
- GEORGE WASHINGTON

"*S*he's coming around now, Colonel."

Sophia recognized the voice: it belonged to the man who had driven the carriage. Her mind began swirling again with images and scenes she could scarcely believe were real. Had she really been rescued from a fate worse than death? Been caught in strong arms before falling? Had it been mere minutes ago? Or days? She could not account for time or distinguish whether it was night or day. But she remembered hands that were blessedly gentle, and a voice that brought soothing relief.

"Open your eyes, Sophia." She heard the voice again, commanding yet kind. The sound of it coming through the darkness reassured her somewhat, and with great effort, she obeyed the order.

Colonel Morgan's figure loomed above her, a dark, shielding presence that cast a shadow over the pew on which she lay. His face began to come into focus as he knelt down beside her, a look of concern radiating from his eyes.

"Sophia," is all he said, but her name on his lips, spoken so softly and tenderly, felt like a reverent caress.

Sophia studied his careworn countenance, at the worry reflected in his tightly knit brow, and then reached up and touched one of the black powder smudges that creased his face. "They came?"

"Yes, they came." He seemed determined to appear strong, to put force in his voice, but exhaustion and concern somewhat impeded his words. "It's... over."

She closed her eyes tight for a moment. "Major Briggs?"

"He won't bother you anymore."

She asked him no questions for his face told her everything. As she took a deep breath of relief, her gaze came to rest on a blood-soaked rag tied around his arm. Her eyes darted back up to his. "You are wounded."

Morgan glanced down at the bandage indifferently as if the injury had already been forgotten. "Only slightly."

Sophia did not bother to offer the sympathy she knew he would detest, but wished she could read in his expression. Had the battle's outcome been decisive? Or unclear? He seemed always the same in victory or defeat—composed, self-assured, and stoic. She closed her eyes again, trying to account for the loss of time and to come to terms with all that had transpired. "What time is it?"

Morgan shrugged. "Around eight."

Sophia blinked. "In the morning?"

"Yes, in the morning. The fight has been over for hours now."

"And your men?" She raised her head and looked around. "How did they fare?"

Morgan's jaw tightened. "They fought bravely, as always." His eyes got that faraway look again. "Most are headed back to safer territory. The worst of the wounded have been taken to nearby homes."

Sophia struggled to sit up when she realized she was probably the sole reason why he remained behind.

"You need to rest." Morgan's voice touched her with its alarm, as he tried to stop her.

"I'm fine now. *You* need to get back to your men."

"It can wait." He seemed not to notice that her clothes were dirty and her hair a mess. He stared at her as if she were a china doll that was fragile and would break at the slightest movement.

"Please, Colonel Morgan. I am fine."

A flash of pain crossed his face as he leaned still closer and studied her intently. With his face only inches from hers, Sophia noticed for the first time the raw agony in his eyes, the look of anguish and torment in his expression. Time seemed to stop, and all movement was suspended as she waited for him to speak.

"My name is Grant," he said at last.

He said nothing more, but clasped her hand in a way that said what words could not. As he helped her sit upright, Sophia stole a look at his eyes, but could read nothing from them now. He revealed only a resolute, determined look, as if he were fighting to control himself, to deny the outward display of any weakness or feelings.

Sophia swallowed hard and gazed at him again. "I would like to know what happened... Grant."

As he sat back in the pew and exhaled, Sophia sensed that he was drained from the weight of responsibility and was exhausted from the fight. Yet with his hand still in hers, she perceived a potent strength, a vibrant force flow into her.

"Very well." He sounded indifferent and calm. "As you

learned, I received a communication to meet you at a designated time and place.

"Yes," Sophia said, earnestly. "And I received the same from you."

Grant paused and looked down into her eyes. "Yes. Except I knew it was not from you."

Sophia blinked in surprise. "Why? How?"

He smiled, his eyes glistening strangely in the morning light. "I told you to never write anything down, Sophia. I knew you wouldn't."

Sophia closed her eyes and nodded, thinking how plain and simple it all appeared now. Grant had planned for a grand deception, while she had done exactly what Briggs had intended…walked blindly into his trap. When she gazed back up at him, his expression spoke volumes even in its silence, implying that the topic need not be discussed.

"Go on," she instructed.

"I arrived at the house at about the same time you did, but from the opposite direction. Briggs had posted four sentries outside so it was impossible to stop you."

"I did not see them," Sophia said almost to herself.

Grant looked at her with pitying tenderness. "My men took care of them while I crept up to the window to assess what was happening inside."

"You heard my conversation with Briggs?" Sophia twisted in the pew so she could view his face more clearly.

"Yes, most of it." Grant spoke now as if to the morning light, without looking at her directly. She might have expected him to gaze warmly into her eyes or at least press her hand a little harder, but he did neither. Sophia's heart plummeted as she came to the conclusion that he perhaps thought her reckless instead of brave.

"But the horse… I mean, I heard you coming."

"That was one of my men. Beck rode up to the porch as

a decoy in case anyone was watching, dismounted, and then I went into the house."

"And pretended to be surprised." Sophia bit her lip in tearless pain as the image of his face came before her.

"Yes. I'm sorry for that, Sophia." His low voice fell soothingly on her ear. "I had to find out how many men were involved before we could make our move."

When his voice cracked, Sophia looked up at his unguarded expression and realized he had suffered as much as she had. The ordeal had required him to be painstakingly thorough, and to be both cautious and bold in correct contrast and proportion.

He had no way of knowing what Major Briggs had planned, and no way of combatting forces unseen. Under the greatest adversity, he had prevailed. The strength it took to do so, while ensuring her safety, made him appear grandly heroic to her. Yet his courage was as inevitable as the rest of his conduct—selfless, daring, and noble.

Sophia took a deep breath and closed her eyes, willing herself to be strong. "Continue."

"When my men heard the carriage coming, they overpowered the driver, and one of them put on his uniform. This church is where we had planned beforehand to rendezvous, so, not being able to communicate with me, he brought you here."

Sophia thought back to how seamlessly it had all worked, when in reality his men had acted on instinct, using the boldness and audacity of their commander as their guide.

"Did Briggs let you go?"

Grant laughed grimly. "No. As soon as you were gone, he informed me that he would take great pleasure in personally delivering me to a prison ship."

Sophia's head jerked up and her eyes met his. "But he told me if I married him, he'd let you go!"

"He had no intention of doing that."

Sophia blinked to stop the images that now raced through her mind. She had been close to throwing away her life in marriage to a man she abhorred—all for nothing. She put her face in her hands and sobbed.

Grant gently pulled away her hands, but his composure for a moment seemed somewhat shaken. "Don't cry. Please don't."

Sophia wiped her tears and gazed up at his weary visage, her eyes lingering on a long, red scratch on his neck. He appeared handsome and gentle and virtuous, like he had nothing to do with flesh and blood, and for a moment she could not speak.

"I want you to forget this night ever happened, Sophia," he said with a tone of gentle solicitude. "It is behind us now."

She nodded. "But how did you get here?"

"My men stormed the house once you were gone. In the firefight, Briggs escaped."

Sophia's breath escaped violently as she looked up at him with fear and surprise.

"Don't worry." He squeezed her hand and continued with a face of unchanging solemnity. "He didn't get away a second time."

Sophia gazed out over his shoulder. "They attacked us here then?"

Morgan didn't answer at first. He stared at the sunbeams that appeared to be held captive in the haze of the church as if recalling the scenes she had not witnessed. "Yes. I had divided my force, so half of my men were already here. Briggs did not comprehend the strength of my force—or my resolve."

"But how did you arrive here before I did?"

"A horse is faster than a carriage—especially when there

is a shortcut." He smiled. "How do you think I got all of these scratches?"

Sophia sighed and leaned back, closing her eyes a moment as she tried to absorb all she had learned. She felt Grant move restlessly in his seat beside her as if he had something more to say, but instead of speaking, he stood and begin to pace.

When she heard him pause, she opened her eyes and found him looking at her with a gaze as tender as ever he had worn for her. Then he turned away and stood with hands on hips, staring at the high windows of the church as they reflected the rays of the brilliant sun.

Sophia looked at his back, and wondered what he was thinking as he silently studied the panes of glass. His shirt emphasized the breadth of his shoulders in the soft sunlight, and his stance revealed a man still ready to fight. The essence of his courage and fortitude glowed, burned, and pulsed in every fiber of his frame.

He appeared to Sophia like a pillar of strength, yet when he spoke his voice held a tremor. "Tell me something, Sophia," he said, with his back still toward her.

"Yes?"

He turned around and regarded her with a troubled expression. "Were you really going to marry Briggs, believing it was the only way to spare my life?"

Sophia paused, but only for a moment. "Of course."

"Why?" He studied her face with a look of mingled hope and uncertainty as if he trying to read his fate in her eyes.

Sophia looked down, unable to meet his gaze as she tried to control the intensity and rhythm of her heartbeat. She had never loved him so well, or desired him so much as when that question was asked.

But when she lifted her eyes and observed the serious and solemn look upon his face, she decided she had to suppress what she had resolved to conceal. Although she thought she had seen signs that he cared for her, she was no longer sure. So she swallowed hard and said something equally as true.

"Because you are esteemed and admired by your men and the citizens. The country could ill afford to lose you now."

She thought she saw a flash of disappointment in his shimmering eyes before he turned his back again. "I see."

A stillness fell upon the room that made Sophia want to scream to fill the silence. "You must think me weak," she murmured, knowing he had contempt for fear and fragility.

"Quite the contrary." He was beside her again, but his hand did not reach for hers, and his manner had become grave and restrained. He even avoided looking at her now, making her heart ache at his sudden indifference. He seemed to be able to curb emotion as a rider would curb a rearing steed—as only a man in absolute control of himself can do.

"But I was so frightened."

"Courage is not the absence of fear." He looked over her head, and seemed to become lost in thought for a moment. When he brought his attention back down to her, she could tell his mind was still elsewhere. "It's bravery in the face of fear. The country owes you a great debt."

He never alluded to his own courage, nor apparently thought of it, evidently feeling neither triumph nor a sense of accomplishment at his victory.

Sophia waited for him to continue, but he seemed intent on listening to the renewed sound of hoof beats outside the stone walls of a church. In another moment a soldier's head appeared in the doorway.

"Colonel Morgan. A dispatch for you, sir."

Morgan turned back to her. "Excuse me a moment. This might be important." His gaze lingered longer than was perhaps proper before he bowed, and strode away.

# CHAPTER 14

*There is a Destiny which has the control of our actions, not to be*
*resisted by the strongest efforts of Human Nature.*
- GEORGE WASHINGTON

*S*ophia picked up a blanket lying on the pew and threw the threadbare cloth across her shoulders as she waited for Grant to return. The morning air was still chilly despite the dazzling display of light streaming in through the windows and the open door.

As the low-toned voices outside came to a stop, she watched a man on horseback salute and snap back to his ramrod-straight cavalryman's seat before taking to the road in a whirl of dust.

A few moments later Grant stepped back through the door, looking troubled and drawn as he studied the missive he held in his hands. Absorbed in his task, he seemed oblivious to Sophia's presence, providing her the opportunity to scrutinize him in wistful silence.

Even with his clothes covered with powdery dust, and his arm still bandaged with the same dirty rag, he reflected a raw and robust vitality. That he was a soldier to his core, Sophia was sure no one could disagree. That she loved him with all her heart, she could no longer pretend to deny.

Grant appeared uneasy as he deliberated upon the communication, his eyes continuing to scan it as if thinking between the words. When he finally looked up, his gaze drifted from Sophia's eyes to something over her shoulder, and his expression turned from one of thoughtful reflection to one of complete alarm.

Sophia watched the blood drain from his stern countenance as he took another step forward. "Have a care, Captain Tate, and leave the lady out of this."

Sophia turned her head just enough to see that Captain Tate had quietly entered behind her through a different door. He remained silent as he stood there, but Sophia saw treachery in his eyes and an expression on his face she knew enough to fear.

"Sophia, step away," Grant said hurriedly, but the warning came a moment too late. Before she could move, Tate lunged and caught her from behind with violent ferocity. Although she struggled and fought, he overpowered her and succeeded in holding her with an unyielding grip.

In another instant he pulled out a long-bladed knife, just as Grant covered the distance to a mere arm's length away.

"Let her go." Grant's commanding voice thundered and reverberated through the empty chambers of the church.

Tate reacted by wrenching Sophia nearer to him and bringing the knife closer to her throat. "Stay where you are, Grant." His voice sounded low and threatening in Sophia's ear. With her eyes tightly closed, she bit her lip to keep from crying out.

Grant's impeccable restraint did credit to him now, as he

casually dropped the hand holding the crumpled paper down by his side.

"I see I got here just in time." Tate laughed. "That communication is about me, isn't it?"

Grant stood breathing heavily, but otherwise showed no sign of duress. "You guess rightly," he said calmly, though his eyes were watchful. "Your deception is now well known throughout the ranks, Captain Tate. There is no escape."

"We'll see about that. How highly do you prize the life of the lady?" He touched the blade of the knife to Sophia's throat and waited for a reaction.

Sophia could barely draw breath as the two men in the room stared at her, one with evil delight—the other with grave concern. Or was it something else she saw in Grant's eyes before she lowered her gaze to the floor?

Grant drew in a long deep breath and let it out slowly. Then he talked distinctly and deliberately as if watching the effect of his words. "If you will permit the exchange of my life for hers, I will esteem it a privilege."

Sophia lifted her eyes and stared at him with a look of mute appeal. His expression now declared something more than mere concern for her, and she had to bite her lip again to keep from whimpering or showing weakness.

"I thought as much." Tate increased the pressure of his grasp. "Call the men off, and I'll let her go when I'm safely out of your reach."

Sophia watched Grant's face to catch a glimpse of what was passing in his mind, but now she could find no trace of that which she sought. It was as if held a secret that his ever-guarded expression dared not betray. She had never witnessed more coolness and courage in a man.

"Let her go *now*, Captain Tate. It will go better for you if you do."

"Oh, no, my friend. I am leaving, and she is going with me."

Grant's gaze shifted to Sophia, and his eyes lingered upon her with penetrating scrutiny, almost as if they were the only ones in the room. In the look he conveyed a message that she read with explicit clearness. *Stay calm and go along for now.*

"For the sake of your life, Captain Tate," Sophia said in a strangled whisper, clinging to the confidence Grant gave her, "do not underestimate the depth of his resolve."

Tate merely laughed. "I believe I understand—better than anyone—the depth of his resolve. But look at him, standing there so powerless." Tate increased his grasp on Sophia as he shifted his weight. "How does it feel, Grant?"

"You are making a big mistake, Lawrence—"

"No, *you* are the one who's made the mistake!" The hostility between the two men pulsed like a tangible force. "You never thought about what it is like to live in your shadow, did you?"

"I gave you every opportunity to prove yourself," Grant said, his expression held motionless as a gun to the head. "You've no one to blame but yourself."

"Oh, I've proved myself, all right. The British are going to make me a colonel, and pay me handsomely for what I've done for them."

"So that's what this is about? Power and money?" Grant had begun to circle around so Tate had to turn to keep him in his sight.

"It's about *respect*!" Tate raised his voice for the first time and there was savagery in it. "Don't move or I'll kill her."

"If you kill her, you'll have no way out."

The idea seemed to enrage Tate even more. "So be it!" he yelled. "She's the reason we were caught! Oh, the two of you had me fooled for a little while, but Briggs and I figured it out."

Sophia closed her eyes again in silent dismay at the mention of Briggs and the realization the two of them had been working together all along.

"Let her go and we'll talk." Grant sounded calm, soothing.

Tate laughed again and this time it sounded fanatical. "No deal, Colonel Morgan, but it is indeed a pleasure to see your concern! Finally I possess something you cannot have." He began to pull Sophia toward the door from which he had entered. "I'm afraid you will never get the opportunity to cherish the bride you have wrested from the arms of another."

When Sophia gathered the courage to look at Grant again, his expression was no longer effectively masked.

"You'll not harm her and live," Grant said, his tone low and threatening. "Depend upon it."

Sophia watched a dreadful calm descend upon Grant's countenance and wondered at the look. When she heard the whisper of another footstep behind her, an instinct that went deeper than thought prepared her for what was to come. Within a heartbeat, Grant lunged forward and grabbed her arm, just as one of his men came up from behind and knocked the knife from Tate's hand.

The speed at which Grant sprang, grasped, and pulled her to safety, startled her. In another swift movement, he pushed her behind him and stood like a mountain between her and Tate. Without thinking, Sophia grabbed a piece of his shirt, and found herself leaning against him for support.

With her gaze attached to Tate, whose arms were being held behind his back, Sophia felt Grant lean down and slowly pull a long, glistening knife from his boot. The muscles in his arm bulged, displaying hard, sinewy, steel-tempered flesh, as he raised the knife high.

Tate closed his eyes seeming to prepare himself for the deathblow, but Sophia grabbed Grant's arm in one swift movement. "Stop! Have mercy."

"Fighting men deserve mercy," he answered, never taking his eyes off his quarry. "Traitors deserve justice."

Sophia felt a tremor shudder through the arm she held. She had seen men angry before, but never anything like this cold, uncontrollable, consuming rage that caused every tautly held muscle in his body to quiver.

He showed as much tendency toward leniency or mercy as a man-eating tiger, and she couldn't help but think of the damage he was capable of inflicting with but one powerful hand. His eyes flashed in such a way that made her believe he did not need the knife to dispose of his foe in one deadly swoop.

"It is for a military court to determine justice," Sophia said, forcefully. "Not you."

Grant stood rigid, his arm still raised as the warring of vengeance and duty continued to shake him. This intensity and ferocity of his character did much to mask his usual calm, quiet, unassuming manner.

"Do not let him goad you into losing your purpose," Sophia said softly. "Remember what we seek here." She pressed his powerful arm with her hand again, imploring him not to hurt the man who so little deserved her mercy.

Grant's eyes remained bright with fury and impatience, but his tone became purposeful as he slowly lowered his arm. "Bind him and post a guard," he told the man holding Tate. "See to it that no one puts a bullet in his head before his trial. He shall hang as a traitor."

Grant walked out the door then, letting it slam closed behind him, but Sophia could hear him outside issuing orders in a strong, thunderous tone. When the talking stopped, there was only a brief pause before he threw the door open again with enough force to pull it off its hinges, and began moving toward her with a long, steady, purposeful stride that dared anyone to get in his way.

Without speaking, he swept her into his arms and held her more tightly than was reasonable or dignified. It was a deceptively gentle embrace for all its searching strength, and for a moment he seemed incapable of doing more than feeling her heart beat against his.

"What are you doing here, Sophia?" he whispered at last. "You should be living your life—not fighting for it."

Sophia closed her eyes and took in the smell of him, the sweat and the leather and the smoke, and knew she could never love as she loved this man. Yet, how could he explain to him what she had only just come to understand herself?

He responded to her silence by tightening his embrace, and Sophia found herself wondering how a mortal man could possess such immense gentleness and such resilient strength.

When a neighing horse punctured the silence, he sighed heavily and let her go with what seemed like deep reluctance, as if he, too, were unsure of what to say or do next.

Turning away, he began to pace. The sound of his boots as they struck the floor caused Sophia to wince at each footstep. "You do not know what to do with me I suppose," she said, after watching him a few moments.

He paused in front of her and nodded, staring as if in deep deliberation. "It is unexpected. And presents a...complication."

Sophia watched his chest rise and fall as he studied her and wondered if his heart pulsed and throbbed as violently as hers. She remembered the swiftness with which he had thrown his body between her and Tate, his unrestrained reflex, and knew he had done so, not as a soldier, but as a man.

"Not so complicated, really," she said, smiling gravely. "You are free to do as you please."

His chest heaved once as if his large heart suddenly twisted in its cage, and his words when he spoke were tender and gentle. "Freed by one hand perhaps, but entrapped by the other, Sophia."

Sophia cocked her head as she studied him, trying to interpret his unreadable thoughts. "Entrapped?" Her tone made it clear that she found it unreasonable of him to act as if she had intentionally set out to entangle him. She turned away, lest he see the anger in her eyes, and heard him take a step forward. One arm soon reached out to encircle her waist and then the other, as he leaned down and whispered in her ear. "I was entrapped the first time I met you, Sophia Adair, and have been so ever since."

He had not surrendered easily, but it appeared he had done so completely. Sophia closed her eyes and took in the feel of his strong arms surrounding her.

"Forgive me for my reticence, Sophia." He sighed. "I cannot rely on a gift of eloquence I do not possess."

Yet when Sophia turned to face him, his expression spoke volumes, saying what words failed to say. He was a man who controlled his emotions and passion, but this time, the admiration and contentment expressed in his eyes was evident.

"Why do you fight it, Grant?" He frowned and turned away, as if he regretted looking weak or vulnerable. He walked to the window, and did not speak or direct to her one glance for a few long moments.

"You must understand I have a duty," he finally said, turning around with his hands on his hips and staring at her as if that explained everything.

"So do I." She put her hands on her hips and met his gaze with one equally as determined.

"You cannot come with me. You must go someplace safe." His voice was no longer gentle, and his words sounded more like an order than a statement.

"I will be safe with you."

Grant stared at her intently, his eyes suffused with a private anguish. "No one knows how grievously untrue that is as well as myself. You must have lost your mind to say such a thing."

"Not my mind. Just my heart." Sophia remained steadfast. "Surely you do not mean to teach me the value of your affection by depriving me of it."

His gaze met hers again with that unfathomable, inscrutable look of his, and for a moment he was silent and preoccupied. "I only wish my affection could be a shield to you." She heard a catch in his voice halfway through, but he finished the sentence bravely. "For your valor in defending your country you should be honored as a patriot—not forced to live as a soldier's bride."

"It is your love I want, Grant—not honors."

As his thoughts seemed to rest on her in quiet abstraction, she unfolded an arm, palm up for the taking. After a moment's hesitation, he reached for it, his strong masculine fingers enclosing around her delicate hand.

"No one can boast as boundless a love as I have for you, Sophia." He paused and swallowed hard. "I only worry that I cannot render myself worthy of the trust you have reposed in me."

Never did the pulse of devotion beat stronger in a human heart, than when she stared into his midnight blue eyes. The expression in them was hopeful, affectionate…promising.

Sophia smiled as the sun poured through the window enveloping them both in a shaft of warm, dazzling light. For a few long moments, the seclusion, the sanctity, and the sun were too magnificent for speech—even though, deep down, they both knew the serenity and tranquility would not last.

Sophia finally broke the spell. "Then I can stay with you? You will except this twist of fate?"

Grant pulled her into his arms and took a long, deep breath. "My darling, who am I to argue with *destiny*?"

# FIND OUT WHAT EVERYONE'S TALKING ABOUT!

*What They Said About the Original Shades of Gray*
**(Now a Trilogy)**

"Rivals Gone With the Wind as my favorite novel of all time. I can think of no better way to describe it." – *Amazon Reviewer*

"I think it is the best Civil War fiction book since Cold Mountain." – *James D. Bibb, Sons of Confederate Veterans, Trimble Camp 1836*

"A classic love story as much as it is a war story." – *Civil War Book Review*

"If you want to read a book you will never forget and will think about for months after reading it, read Shades of Gray. It took my breath away. Honestly, you will not sleep."

"My house is a mess, my sink is piled high with dishes and my husband ate watermelon for dinner because I could not put down Shades of Gray. Could. Not. Put. Down. Honestly, this book completely captivated me and left me emotionally drained. I loved it!!!"

"I've not been much of a reader and was given Shades of Gray. I've read it five times and fall in love every time I read it. Because of you I have developed a love for reading."

"It is now 1 a.m. cause I couldn't put down my I-pad with your delicious novel. Thank you for the pleasure you afforded this 81 year old."

"Wonderful, fabulous book! I seldom reflect back on a book, but this one has haunted me since I finished it at 2 a.m."

"Could hardly work or sleep until I read the last page."

"Lost a lot of sleeping reading this one. Too good to put down! Made me laugh. Made me cry. Awesome book!"

"I loved this novel. Still crying, but I laughed just as much as I cried."

"Bravo! One of the best books I have read on the Civil War. Absolutely could not put it down. Please do not stop writing."

"Excellent book. Well-developed characters. Edge of your seat suspense."

"I can't remember having such a heavy heart and crying so much since reading Gone with the Wind. Thank you!"

"Loved. Loved. Needs to be made into a movie."

"I'm not usually one for Civil War era books, but I've got to say you really got me on this one. I LOVE it!"

"Oh my, I let the world go on around me and could hardly put it down. Every free moment, every break at work. LOVED IT!!!"

"As a history buff I have never read a more compelling novel with a Civil War setting. Brilliant. I was SEEING events rather than reading words."

"I was completely lost and spellbound by the realistic story. Without hesitation I must say Noble Cause now ranks equally with Gone With The Wind."

"Though a male I liked it, and recommended it to my wife."

"I stayed up until 2 a.m. two nights in a row because I couldn't put it down. It was a book that I couldn't wait to read, yet I didn't want it to end!"

"This book has touched me more than any other I have ever read. I cried, laughed, and then cried some more. Thank you for such an amazing and touching story."

"If someone said I could only ever have one book for the rest of my life either of these [Shades of Gray or Noble Cause] would be my pick. Thank you."

"I know a book is very good when I think about it after I complete the book, and I cannot start another one right away. Five star rating for sure."

This book absolutely ripped my heart out. Superb. Thank you for such a moving, believable love story."

"I have not read a romance novel in probably 10 years. Your book was so good for my soul."

**Don't Miss Out! Order Today!**

**NEW SHADES OF GRAY TRILOGY**

DUTY BOUND
HONOR BOUND
GLORY BOUND
COMPLETE CIVIL WAR TRILOGY

## LET'S BE FRIENDS!

GET EXCLUSIVE JESSICA JAMES MATERIAL

Building a relationship with my readers is the best part about being an author. I occasionally send newsletters with details on new releases, special offers and other bits of news relating to my books.

Sign up for my Newsletter for free content. www.sub-scribepage.com/jessicajamesnews

Email Jessica@JessicaJamesBooks.com

Author Website: www.JessicaJamesBooks.com

History and Travel Blog: www.PastLaneTravels.com

Goodreads: https://www.goodreads.com/jessicajames

Facebook Fan Page: www.facebook.com/romantichistorical-fiction

BookBub: www.bookbub.com/authors/jessica-james

# ABOUT THE AUTHOR

JESSICA JAMES is a multi-award winning author of historical fiction and military suspense. Her novels appeal to both men and women, and are featured in library collections all over the United States, including Harvard and the U.S. Naval Academy.

By weaving the principles of courage, devotion, and dedication into each book, she attempts to honor the unsung heroes of the American military—past and present—and to convey the magnitude of their sacrifice and service.

# LACEWOOD

***Sometimes love is too powerful for one lifetime...***

"Found them!" The sheriff backed his lean frame out of the window and waved a ring of keys before heading toward the gate. As he stomped through the dense grass he pointed to the ground. "Careful, there's broken glass everywhere, and who-knows-what hidden in the weeds."

Katie stopped and looked down at her open-toed sandals. "What exactly do you mean by, *who-knows-what*?" She lifted one foot and then the other. "Like snakes?"

"Could be." He nodded. "But don't worry, they won't hurt you...unless you step on them, of course."

"Thanks," Katie mumbled as she concentrated on placing her feet where his had been.

As he stood at the gate, the sheriff inspected each key, and finally held one up. "I think it's this one." With a little jiggling and jostling, the rusty padlock opened and the chain fell away. The sheriff pushed on the gate, but it didn't move at first. After a few hard shakes, the hinges let loose, emitting a wailing, high-pitched screech that made Katie feel a bit unwelcome.

"Follow me," he said. "Watch out for loose bricks."

Walking carefully along the neglected path, Katie stepped to the side to touch the bark of one of the trees towering over the front yard. "I've seen these white trees before, but I don't know what they're called." The trunk displayed a distinctive fusion of creams, grays, and browns, but the limbs above were a smooth, snowy white that stood out vividly against the brilliant blue sky.

The sheriff stopped and turned. "They're sycamores. See how the bark forms a lacy pattern at the bottom? Back in the old days they called it lacewood." He turned and bounded up the steps while Katie ran her fingertips over the intricate design. "It's beautiful," she said, under her breath. "*Lacewood*."

"Of course, another common name for the tree here-abouts is ghostwood," the sheriff quipped over his shoulder while he searched through the keys. "But that wouldn't make a very good name for a house, now would it?"

Katie lifted her eyes from the multicolored bark at the bottom to the skeletal limbs overhead. Even in broad daylight the trees appeared ghostly, with budding branches reaching out like bony fingers. Yet the unusual color was so beautiful it dispelled any notions of apprehension or fear.

After one last look at the patterns on the base of the nearest tree, Katie turned to follow the sheriff. The stately pillars bookmarking the wide veranda added a grace and charm to the otherwise run-down property. She put her hand on one of them as she walked by, and jumped back when the paint fragmented and showered the ground.

Ignoring the flaws, Katie focused instead on the long-forgotten majesty of bygone days. Yes, the outward appear-ance suggested deterioration and decay, but the dignity of the place remained intact as far as she was concerned.

The sheriff triumphantly held up an old skeleton key before sticking it in the lock. The thick wooden door creaked open noisily—some might say mournfully—after the sheriff gave it several hard shoves with his shoulder.

Clearing the doorway of spider webs with a few swipes of his hand, he walked in without a moment's hesitation. Katie, on the other hand, eyed the space above her and on each side before cautiously following him through. When she stepped across the threshold, she let out her breath in one long, "W-o-w!"

"Welcome to Lacewood," the sheriff said. "These fourteen-foot ceilings really hit you when you first walk in, don't they?"

Katie merely nodded as she gaped at the antique chandelier overhead. Though time and dust had dimmed the sparkle, the elaborate detail suggested it was made of the finest crystal. It was a work of art, breathtaking even in its current condition.

Tearing her gaze away, Katie next feasted her eyes on the two pillars marking the arched entrance to a wide hallway running the length of the house. "I've never seen columns inside a house before," she said, almost to herself.

"It's extra support, I guess," the sheriff said. "This foyer is as big as some houses. On the left, through those double doors, is the ballroom."

"Ballroom?" Katie surveyed the wide plank floors, bare of everything but layers of dust. Decorative woodwork displaying quality artistry and craftsmanship bordered the walls and led the eye to the grand staircase off to the right. A sweeping bottom step narrowed and curved up to the second floor, as glamorous and majestic as the movie set of *Gone with the Wind*.

Katie moved forward, hesitant yet excited. Despite the decades of dirt and decay, she felt a welcoming presence here, a warm and friendly vibe. Sure, the house conveyed the impression it was too far gone to revive. But Katie preferred to think it was slumbering, perhaps dreaming of the day when someone would open the windows, allowing fragrant breezes to drift through the hallways and radiant sunlight to stream into the rooms.

Making her way over to the staircase, Katie touched the rich wood of the bannister, worn smooth by centuries of hands. *Whose? And where did they go? Why did they leave?*

The peace of the house and its timeless beauty unlocked something in Katie, making a prickly sensation race up her spine. There were stories here. Long-forgotten, and hidden just out of her reach. Were they to be lost forever?

Katie's thoughts returned to her grandmother's house. Did people still live there? Did they know about the laughter that once echoed through the halls, the ageless wisdom once passed on within its walls? Did they care?

Turning in a circle, Katie studied the room again. Faded wallpaper curled in strips above the dusty wainscoting, but the walls themselves appeared sturdy. Down the hall a set of double glass doors stood open in apparent welcome. On the far side of the entryway, and dominating the wall, a mammoth fireplace yawned beneath an ornately carved hearth. Katie's attention was immediately drawn to a painting of a woman in nineteenth century dress that hung prominently over the mantel.

"Who is *she*?"

The sheriff turned to the dusty, sun-bleached portrait in the heavy Victorian-era frame. "One of the previous owners, they say." He shrugged. "The family history kind of got lost with the house. Everyone around here calls her the Widow of Lacewood."

Katie stood spellbound, riveted on the portrait, unable to speak or even move. The woman was dressed completely in black, but the magnificence of the gown gave the impression of sophistication and class. Her chin was slightly elevated as if to project strength, yet there was more than a hint of sorrow and pain in her eyes.

"She seems so sad." Katie spoke without removing her gaze. "And so young. How could she be a widow?"

The sheriff had already started to walk away, but he turned back to the painting. "Not sure, but they say she never remarried. She's the one out in the cemetery, too, I reckon."

Katie's heart suddenly struggled to beat, as if her blood had turned to molasses and couldn't flow. The anguish in the woman's expression held her spellbound. She could see the pain. *Feel* a heart ripped apart. Something was missing that could never be replaced.

Katie had felt such loss before. In a way, that's why she was here.

**ORDER LACEWOOD TODAY!**

- Winner of the 2020 John Esten Cooke Award for Southern Fiction
- Finalist 2020 Greater Detroit RWA Booksellers Best Award contest
- Finalist 2020 HOLT Medallion Award